PACIFIC

PURSUIT

Leigh Jarrett

Published by Steambath Press
An LJ M/M Romance

Paperback published July 2023
ISBN-13: 978-1-998008-12-4

Chapter One | Peter

Peter had a secret. It had nothing to do with his thriving real estate business or the many close friendships he'd developed over the years. Nothing that simple. Even his rocky childhood wasn't a secret. He openly shared the tragedies that had shaped his life. This secret—it was something buried deep inside his soul. Something he could never let out into the world.

It was the kind of secret that could tear his carefully constructed reality into pieces.

His love for his wife, Louise, had been real, but he'd had other thoughts running around in his head the whole thirty-seven years he'd been married to her. He'd never shared them with anyone.

How could he? He wasn't even sure he hadn't made them up somehow. The life he'd had with Louise had been difficult. It was no wonder his mind had wandered.

After they were first married, they'd tried for years to have children. Naturally and through in vitro fertilization. Through it all, he hadn't even been sure he wanted to have kids. The thought of having a family, a whole group of people relying on him terrified him. Plus, it didn't match with the dreams of a different kind of life that he often fantasized about for himself.

Louise had been desperate for children. Almost to the point of being obsessed with the life she saw herself leading with him. The plan had been for Louise to be a stay-at-home mom. She'd never pursued a career of her own. After five years of trying to conceive, they'd adopted a son. It only partially fulfilled the life Louise wanted. She still longed for a child of her own.

They'd kept trying.

It wasn't to be.

Through their years together, they'd dealt with numerous hardships. Miscarriages, bouts of extreme depression for them both, a house fire where they lost everything, and bankruptcy.

The bankruptcy. They had lost their home for a second time.

Then their sweet son, Samuel, at the age of seventeen, got himself hooked on heroin and fentanyl. Samuel hadn't even finished high school when he went to his first rehabilitation center. He had four relapses until he finally broke free of the destructive drugs' clutches.

Now Louise was gone; uterine cancer. And his life was his own again. His son was thirty-two, living a life of his own. In recovery twelve years. Married with children. The whole package.

Peter had never imagined he would be a grandfather one day. And he was a good one. He doted on those kids, Michael and Julie. He was all in, whether babysitting, taking them out to the park, or attending their soccer games. Those children and their parents were his life.

But after Louise's death, he'd wandered aimlessly in his thoughts. Not able to hold a string of them cohesively in his head. His relationship with his family had stumbled.

They had given him space while he worked through his grief. And the grief was deep. He'd known Louise since he was eighteen years old. Louise, sixteen. They'd spent a lifetime together. The chasm in his heart had been broad enough to swallow him whole.

His work had suffered. His friendships had suffered. His

apathy soon had friends drifting away from him. All except one. His best friend Maxwell Carter. They'd known each other since middle school. Got themselves in a good amount of trouble in their youth. Sneaking out for midnight bike rides to toilet paper bullies' houses. Smoking cigarettes out back of Maxwell's shed. Setting off a small explosion in their chemistry lab. Drinking rum in the tent his parents had let them set up in the backyard until they were sick all over the lawn. They'd been terrors.

They'd also been there for each other no matter what. Maxwell had been by his side throughout Louise's battle with cancer. He'd been a sounding board for Peter's anguish. He'd provided counsel when he'd been struggling with what would happen after she was gone. The nuts and bolts in the aftermath of someone passing away.

Most importantly, he'd been a shoulder to cry on.

Not once had Maxwell turned him away. Said he was in the middle of something. There was no *phone back later* or *come back tomorrow*. Maxwell had dropped everything when Peter needed him. Much to the chagrin of Maxwell's wife. His worst ill-timing? Maxwell had made his apologies and ducked out of their wedding anniversary dinner because Peter had phoned him in tears.

Peter turned off his computer. He still felt bad about that. He knew when their wedding anniversary was. He had been Maxwell's best man. It had slipped his mind in his moment of distress. Maxwell had shown up at his door, led him to the sofa, and held him while he cried.

That had been ten months ago. His heart was healing.

Life was returning to normal.

He pulled on his coat. He was running late. Tonight was his son's recovery birthday. He'd be receiving his twelve-year chip. Family and friends were invited to attend. It would only take him twenty minutes to get to the church basement where the ceremony would be held.

He had eighteen minutes.

The winter sun was long gone, and the roads were slick with ice. But his Range Rover had little trouble getting him to his destination safely. His business as a real estate agent had turned around ten years back. He'd made a name for himself through hard work and a bit of luck. Big-ticket sellers had started to seek him out to sell their properties. The money started rolling in after that. Now he had a crew of assistants that made his life a lot easier. They'd been the only thing holding his business together while he mourned the loss of his wife.

By chance, the meeting was late to start. Peter had enough time to grab a coffee and find his seat beside Samuel and his wife Laurel.

"Nick of time, Dad," Samuel said.

"Paperwork."

Samuel reached across Laurel, smiled, and patted Peter's knee. "Glad you made it."

"Wouldn't miss it." Peter flashed Samuel what he hoped was an expression of pride. Samuel leaned back and Peter caught sight of the man on the other side of him. Ryan. Maxwell's son. Their two sons had been inseparable from the time they were both in diapers.

He and Maxwell had nothing on the trouble Samuel and Ryan had gotten themselves into. Amongst other antics, fifteen years old, they had *borrowed* Maxwell's car and driven to the Okanagan. Their excuse: they wanted to go swimming somewhere hot.

It had been Ryan who alerted Peter to Samuel's addiction.

He'd been so worried about his best friend that he risked their lifelong friendship to ensure Samuel received help. Samuel had been aggressively angry at Ryan for many months. With time, they'd worked it out and gone back to being each other's safe place.

Next to Ryan sat another man. Ryan kept turning to talk to him. Samuel kept leaning across Ryan to be in on the conversation. Peter recognized the man.

Danny Miller. A young, energetic real estate agent who had taken the market by storm. He hadn't realized Samuel had become friends with him. He must know him through Ryan.

The meeting started with the opening readings. The chairperson said they'd be foregoing a topic to leave enough time to celebrate a significant birthday.

They dimmed the lights and launched straight into *sharing* after that.

Peter looked in the direction of each voice and listened to the stories unfolding. Stories of heartache: loss of family and friends. Stories of hardship: homelessness and violence. Stories of hope: recovery and reconnection. At times, Peter was brought to tears.

He shifted in his seat as the lights were brought back up. The man he knew was Samuel's sponsor Jacob took the floor. Samuel jumped to his feet, grinning, to stand beside him.

Jacob's words took Peter on a roller coaster of emotions. He'd heard the story before, but each time he bore witness to the details of the struggle his son had fought through to make his way to recovery, it tore at his heart. They were important words. The types of words that would give those gathered in that room some optimism, that they could turn their lives around.

Samuel spoke next.

His son was an inspiration.

There had come a time when Samuel couldn't remain in their family home. The fighting, the slurring and nodding off, the destruction—the chaos. Peter looked at his hands. His kind, intelligent, creative baby boy had been given no choice but to find refuge in the city's shelters while waiting for his next trip to rehab. The guilt still haunted him. But Maxwell, a drug and alcohol counselor had explained to him that Samuel needed to desperately want recovery before he had any chance of reaching it. Protecting him at home was just enabling his addiction.

The pride poured out of Peter. The man speaking of his recovery was strong, resilient, and confident. He'd known three versions of his son. The carefree, innocent child. The young man in the depths of addiction and misery. And this man striding forward through life.

This man here—this was the son he liked best.

He clapped with thundering force as Samuel was handed his twelve-year chip.

The meeting closed out and most people made their way to the door. Some stayed behind to congratulate Samuel, including his son's best friend.

Ryan turned from Samuel and spotted Peter. As usual, he was full of enthusiasm and a glimmer of glee. Few things could throw Ryan off his naturally sunny disposition.

He reached forward.

"Mr. Anderson," Ryan said as he shook Peter's hand. "Nice to see you here."

"Wouldn't miss it."

"Thought you'd be working on that Sanderson sale."

"They decided to think about the purchase of the property overnight."

Ryan winked at him. "Famous last words. I've worked with them before. Six in the morning … awoken by a call from them. Christmas Day another time."

Peter smirked. The Sandersons *did* have a reputation in the real estate world of Victoria, BC. A world Ryan belonged to. Ryan had always been interested in what his best friend Samuel's dad did for a living. He thought it was glamorous. The allure of expensive cars and suits, driving rich rich clients who were looking for their next multi-million-dollar property.

He'd been swept up in the illusion.

Ryan had done well enough for himself as a mid-level agent. Enough to support a family along with his wife. They had three children. Two, five, and eight. They were a handful.

The man that had been sitting on Ryan's left approached them.

"Danny." Peter extended his arm, hand open. Ryan returned to Samuel's side.

Danny shook his hand. "Peter."

Now, Danny *was* living the high-end dream. Upscale house, lavish lifestyle, and an endless string of men on his arm. Danny had the intellect and sales savvy to turn a sour deal sweet. A rocky one smooth. An impossible one lucrative. Plus, he had the looks. People were drawn to him.

Danny was gorgeous. With his neatly trimmed dark hair and sexy, stubble beard … Danny was pure sex in a well-tailored suit.

Even Peter had to admit that.

That damned secret of Peter's resurfaced as he looked at Danny. Over the years, he'd spent hours walking the back streets—just looking. His desire nearly drove him to approach the men gathered there looking for *dates*. Danny was far braver than he could ever be.

It was no secret Danny was gay.

"I hadn't realized Samuel was your son," Danny said.

"I hadn't realized you knew him."

"We met through Ryan."

"Thought that might be the case." Peter crossed his arms. "Have you known Samuel long?"

"Quite a few years. We met at Ryan's engagement party. He was very upfront about being two years into his recovery." Danny chuckled. "I tried to buy him a drink."

Peter wasn't sure what to say to that. Had Danny tried to pick up his son? They looked as though they were about the same age. Samuel had met his future wife at that party.

"Glad you're here to support him," Peter said.

"He's been a good friend. Puts up with my crap."

Danny didn't seem like the kind of guy who would have crap to put up with. He acted so put together. And his reputation was impeccable. He was a powerful force in the real estate industry.

"Better get back to him." Danny smiled at Peter. "It was nice chatting with you."

"Yeah, ah … you too."

That was the best he could come up with to say. Danny's smile had disarmed him. Flustered him. Danny meant it when he smiled at you. There was no pretending for the sake of being friendly. The curve of his lips was accompanied by an alluring gleam in his stunning hazel eyes.

Peter's secret bounced around in his mind.

And he didn't know what the hell to do with it.

Chapter Two | Danny

Danny tucked his hands into the pockets of his suit pants and turned back to Samuel. This was his day. He was incredibly proud of his friend. Twelve years. Ten years since they'd met.

He pounded Samuel's back with the flat of his hand.

"Okay, buddy … I gotta go. Congrats again."

Samuel turned and hugged him. "Thanks for coming."

Danny smirked. "Had nowhere else to be. Slow night."

"Off on the prowl after this?" Samuel stepped away and smiled.

"It is Saturday night after all."

"I'd offer to be your wingman, but I'm not in the mood to be groped by some guy." He hooked a thumb in his wife's direction. "Plus, Laurel might disapprove if I liked it."

"Leaves more groping for me."

Samuel crossed his arms. "Be careful."

Danny patted Samuel's cheek. "Always am."

"You off to that real estate convention next week?"

"Yeah." Danny sighed. "Not looking forward to it."

"You're upset about going to Las Vegas? Wish I could go."

"Pretty sure high school schoolteachers weren't invited." Danny's phone buzzed in his pocket. He lifted it out and looked at the screen. "Duty calls. Maybe I'll see you tomorrow."

Danny slipped into business mode as he answered the call. One of his fellow agents had an offer for a 2.4 million dollar home Danny had listed. He should be able to wrap up the negotiations before he had to catch a plane to Las Vegas on

Monday morning.

His Saturday night was likely ruined, though.

He slipped into his Mercedes SUV and brought the engine to life. He turned off the radio and turned on the heat. "What number are we starting with?"

It was still dark when Danny opened his eyes. He rolled over. Saturday night hadn't been a complete bust. He'd headed to his clients' and waited for the offer from the buyer's agent. His clients countered. The buyer's counteroffer had come back an hour later. His client had accepted.

The rest could be done in the morning.

He'd headed for the closest gay bar.

"Hey," the blond bombshell beside him whispered. Tommy. They'd slept together before maybe five months back. He was fun to play with. Nothing more. Danny hadn't been in a committed relationship for almost six years. He had no intention of starting now.

Dominique had brought him nothing but heartache. Shattered every confidence he had in investing his heart in what he thought was a loving relationship. Dominique had cheated on him. Multiple times. At no time had they agreed to an open relationship, but Dominque had been treating what they had together as if they'd talked it through and agreed to one.

His excuse: he was a free spirit that shouldn't be contained.

Danny stroked Tommy's chin then moved closer. He took Tommy's lips with his own. This here—this is what he loved now. The spark of desire as it fired up in one's belly. He ran his fingers into Tommy's hair and deepened the kiss. Tommy's hand came to rest on his bare hip.

And they were off to the races.

When they finished, they were sweaty and heaving—and laughing.

Tommy really was fun.

"Dude, that was awesome," Tommy said and slapped his hand to his forehead. After a few moments of silence, he sat up. "But I have to head out. I have to work in the morning."

"Still at Café Espresso?"

"I'm managing it now."

"Nice."

"Great seeing you again, Danny." Tommy pulled on his underwear after he located them on the floor. His pants were next to cover his sleek, muscular frame. "Can I call you?"

Danny sighed. He hated to do this to the guy. They'd had fun. Conversation *and* sex. Who knew what else he'd discover under that charm and sexy blond hair? He'd never know.

"Let's leave it to chance," Danny answered. "I'm sure we'll run into each other again."

Tommy furrowed his brow. "Sure … yeah."

Danny pulled the sheet over his face when he heard his front door close behind Tommy. The silk material smelled of sweat and sex. He just wanted to hide from the world.

Sleep didn't find him again. He was too wired from his night of fulfilling a handful of his desires. 7 am, he padded to the kitchen and started the coffee pot. It felt like a pancake morning.

He pulled the fridge open. And bacon.

Then he'd hit the gym.

Coffee and food filling his gut, he headed downstairs to his home gym. His trainer would be arriving in 5 minutes. He hoped he hadn't eaten too much. Sometimes, his trainer would go hard on him. Try to break him. The sound of the sliding glass door meant she had arrived.

He silenced his phone.

"Ready, princess?" she asked as she strode into the gym.

Damn.

It was going to be one of her more brutal sessions. She had Danny tuned like an Olympic athlete. He appreciated that. The men he slept with appreciated that. At thirty-four, he was as fit as someone ten years younger. She started him on the treadmill.

He could run for miles, and she knew it. Despite the speed and incline, he powered through. She finally released him and moved him on to free weights. His muscles were burning with each repetition. She watched him with that glint in her eye that scared him to death.

She tapped him on the shoulder.

"Squats. Three-ninety. Three sets. Twelve reps."

Jeezus. She's trying to kill me.

Danny loaded on the weights. He was starting to regret his hearty breakfast. But he managed. She would never push him further than he was capable of lifting. She was brutal but she was also a professional. She had been on the USA Olympic weightlifting team for two games running.

He completed the reps.

"You had enough?"

"Yes, ma'am."

She threw a towel at him. "Do some cooling down and stretches."

Danny dropped the weights to the floor. He pulled the towel off his shoulder and sat on the mat. The stretching felt good. He let his heart rate slow before heading to the shower room.

"Thanks," he called over his shoulder.

"See you on Tuesday?"

"No, I'll be away. Conference. I'll be back by Thursday."

"Thursday then."

"Yeah, see you." Danny wandered into the white-tiled room that doubled as a large open shower. He unmuted his phone and set it on the counter, stripped off his shorts and tank top, and turned on the shower. The hot water felt glorious. His mind turned to men. Men he'd slept with.

Men who had caught his eye.

He smirked.

Samuel's dad was certainly pleasing to look at. A sexy, silver fox he'd seen at open houses. They'd shared a few pleasantries, and been at the opposite ends of some negotiations, but they were adversaries. They were two of a handful of agents at the top of their game.

Danny started in on his hair. Peter had an angular jaw that Danny found mouthwatering and high cheekbones. His lips were ample. Great for kissing. Even better to watch wrapped around your cock. And those eyes … goddamn if their steel-blue intensity didn't drill into your soul.

Stop it.

Samuel's dad.

He soaped up his body. Tommy settled in his imagination, lying in his bed. His hands above his head cuffed together to the headboard. A ball gag in his mouth. He'd driven Tommy to distraction last night with the leather loop of a short crop. Dragged it all up and down his skin.

Played with him until he begged for release.

His thoughts broke as his phone rang. He rolled his eyes. The problem with being a real estate agent is you were always on call. He scrubbed the sweat from his skin, quickly toweled off, and opened his voicemail. His clients from last night were anxious to have the signed sale contract in their hands. He had intended to drive it over in the afternoon. Now was fine, though.

The commission on 2.23 million dollars went a long way when it came to inconvenience. It was more money than most people made in a year at a good job.

He was averaging 16 of those sales a year.

He donned his uniform. An extravagant, tailored navy-blue suit and crisp white shirt. He left it open at the neck. It was the weekend after all. His diamond-encrusted cufflinks were still a go.

Danny slid into his car. All he needed was the contract in an embossed folder and a congratulations package. There would be no *Sold* sign to put on the lawn of this house. There had never been a *For Sale* sign. Homes in this range didn't like their business advertised.

A limited-release bottle of wine and an expensive charcuterie gift basket always brought a smile to his buyers' faces, though. He set them on the passenger seat.

It was a short drive to the home. Down the street in his neighborhood. He'd known the sellers for years. He made a point of introducing himself to all his neighbors. Didn't drop that he was a real estate agent to start with. That came later. Not until he was invited over for a drink, and they asked what he did for a living. Then he was very casual about it. But the seed had been planted.

Weekends like this were a dream.

Then it would be Monday.

He sighed as he pulled into the driveway. It was a necessary evil, but he wasn't looking forward to going to Las Vegas. Dominique would be there. He was at every convention. Danny would've moved on with his life if Dominique hadn't made it so awkward every time they met.

Dominique had it in his head that Danny should be open to

having sex with him. That they had shared so much together. It bordered on creepy. The way Dominique fawned over him.

He threw his car door open and headed for the walk. He appreciated the heated drive and walkway that kept any kind of ice buildup at bay.

The clients were more than thrilled with his attention to detail and the savvy way he had discreetly found a qualified buyer and negotiated the final sale price.

They offered him a glass of wine, but it was too early in the day for him to imbibe. He left them with a promise to find them a property to call their new home. The buyer had agreed to a generous four-month possession date for a shift of thirty-thousand dollars in the price.

The Pacific coast of Canada wasn't known for getting much snow unless you were on the mainland. On Vancouver Island it was rare, but it was snowing as Danny drove home.

Once back under his own roof, he flicked on the fireplace and settled into his sofa with a blanket. He flipped open his eBook reader and immersed himself in the gay male mystery he'd started the week before. Reading was a passion of his.

Spare time was rare, but he grabbed it where he could.

Danny already had a couple of properties in mind for his client. There was no need to spend time on it now. Properties over 3 million didn't tend to fly off the market with any kind of haste. He'd put in a few calls in the morning before he left for the airport.

Right now, the cozy mystery of Waterford Moors was calling.

The next morning was rushed, as usual. Word had gotten around that his clients had sold and were looking for a new property. He ended up fielding a tidal wave of calls with options.

His email filled up with listings. Some suitable. Some absolutely not. He frowned at his phone screen as the taxi driver hurtled down the highway. Some of the realtors were chancing their arms. He deleted an email. A million-dollar fixer-upper? Really?

They pulled up outside departures at the airport and the taxi driver lifted his luggage from the trunk. It was a bright, clear, sunny day. Hopefully, the same in Las Vegas. It was only slightly warmer there in winter than in Victoria. He'd packed appropriately. Lighter clothes for during the warmer part of the day and he had already donned a winter coat for nighttime.

He boarded the plane and stuffed his carry-on luggage into the overhead compartment. It contained toiletries and enough clothes to suffer through for three days. Couldn't be too careful when it came to airlines. The suit he was wearing could be cleaned at the hotel if need be. The rest of his belongings were in his checked baggage. Hopefully, destined for Las Vegas.

He slipped out of his winter coat, did up his seatbelt, and draped the coat over his lap.

Danny closed his eyes and waited for the eventual take-off of the aircraft. People were still bustling their way to their seats. Someone dropped into the seat beside him. They brushed Danny's forearm with their elbow. He popped his eyes open when the fellow traveler spoke.

"Hey. Danny." Peter adjusted his body in his seat and fiddled with his seatbelt. Within moments, Danny was shoulder to shoulder, practically thigh to thigh with the man who had briefly drifted through the start of a fantasy sequence he'd been entertaining in the shower.

"Peter. What are the chances?"

"Pretty high. Half the plane are estate agents." Peter shifted in his seat to face Danny. "Heard about the Carmichael sale. Nice work."

"Thanks. Now to find them somewhere new that suits their very specific tastes."

"There are a few I can think of off the top of my head."

"Me too. I've already contacted the agents. Viewings are set for Thursday."

"You work fast."

Danny licked his lips as the plane rumbled to life. He hated flying.

"The sooner I get them settled, the sooner I can take a break. I've been planning a trip to Italy for months. Just waiting for the right time."

"I went last spring. Beautiful country. Where are you thinking of going?"

"Campania."

"Naples?"

"Positano."

"Nice. Gorgeous coastline."

"I just want to go and relax and soak up the atmosphere."

"You deserve it. You've been working hard. It's only January and you already have two sales under your belt. Not sure how you manage it."

"Perseverance and connections."

"Yeah, connections. You have a reputation." Peter smiled. "People like you."

Danny grinned. "My boyish charm."

Peter settled back in his seat. "You are by no means a boy."

Danny's eyebrows rose. Was Peter flirting with him? By Samuel's account, his parents had been married for over thirty-five years. Peter had to be at least sixty. Late bloomer?

"You've been doing well too," Danny said. "Water views

seem to be your specialty."

"Funny how that kind of happened."

Danny gripped the armrest as the plane rose into the air. In just 2 hours, they would have a layover in Calgary for 2 hours. Another 2 hours and they would be in Vegas. A flight of 2s.

He could grit his teeth through each leg of the journey.

"You don't like flying?" Peter asked.

Danny peered over at Peter. "Hate it."

"Does talking help?"

"Some. It takes my mind off the fact we are forty-thousand feet in the air."

"I brought a book. I could read it aloud."

"What kind of book?"

"It's a mystery."

Danny was about to object but listening to a story in the genre he preferred might calm him down. He smiled. Peter was old enough to be his father. Storytime with Peter.

He laughed.

"Might earn us a few looks."

Peter leaned toward him. "I'll talk quietly."

Danny shrugged. "Can't hurt."

He nearly fell asleep to the sound of Peter's voice. If he wasn't so invested in the story unfolding, he might have ended up snoring on Peter's shoulder.

The storytime idea worked.

They landed in Calgary much sooner than Danny expected. The reading had taken his mind off the fear that usually permeated his every thought while in the air.

They needed to transfer to a different plane. Peter was the first to stand. He reached for the overhead bin to retrieve his belongings. Danny was left to stare at Peter's midriff. His dark-grey suit jacket was open. A light blue dress shirt hid his abs and chest. The man was fit for his age.

Danny's gaze wandered.

He was intrigued.

Had Peter been flirting with him?

Peter hustled off down the aisle leaving Danny to extract himself. He half expected to find Peter waiting for him in the departure lounge. He even looked for him.

Peter was nowhere in sight.

Danny peered down at his ticket on his phone. He needed to find the next departure gate. He knew his way around the Calgary airport well. His gate was down the next arm in the cog.

It only took him a few minutes to wander down there.

Scanning the seating area, he spotted Peter, his nose back in his book. Danny took a seat in the row behind him and at the opposite end. Whatever connection they had made on the first leg of the flight had passed. He opened his email app and flipped through the listings for the homes that were fresh on the market. He'd need to see them first before he showed them to his client.

After he finished that, Danny put an earbud in one ear and listened to an audiobook. Peter had put him in the mood to be read to. He closed his eyes.

The announcement soon came over the speakers that they were boarding. He hoped Peter would be seated beside him again, but he wasn't surprised when it was someone else.

During this leg of the trip, Danny decided to do some work. He had some irons in the fire he needed to rotate and poke into some embers. He retained his laptop and set himself up on the small fold-down table. His task, selling himself and his services without being obvious.

It was an art.

An art he'd perfected.

He opened a software program he used to track leads and checked his notes for the four potential clients who were on the fence about selling. One couple: their twin boys were headed to university on the far side of the country. Maybe it was time to downsize. He had an upscale townhouse that wasn't going to last long. A park down the road for their dog, Sparky.

He worded his message carefully. It had to be their idea. He just needed to present them with a property he had *stumbled* across ... and how he'd thought of them.

Looks good.

Next.

He worked his way through his list. Once finished, he powered down and shut his laptop, leaned his head back, and closed his eyes. He was tired.

The plane touched down in Vegas.

Danny packed up and joined the throng of passengers headed for the luggage turnstile. He thanked the airline gods when he saw his luggage slide onto the conveyor.

He was lucky enough to get a taxi with a few other estate agents. They were all going to the same place. No need to take separate cabs.

He dumped his luggage on the floor inside his hotel room, pressed the door closed, struggled out of his suit jacket, and headed to the washroom. A quick drain of his bladder then he was back in the main room. He hit the bed with a thud and a bounce. He barely pulled a pillow under his head when he passed out. The conference's welcome dinner wasn't until 8 pm.

Plenty of time to sleep and *play* before then.

It was Vegas after all.

Chapter Three | Danny

Danny's alarm on his phone sounded at 4:30 pm. He still had three and a half hours until dinner. He rolled over and opened a gay dating app on his phone. There was plenty of time for a tumble and a shower before he had to head down to the banquet hall.

Quite a few guys were popping up in the vicinity near enough they must be in the hotel. Real estate agents were predominantly male. Offered a lot of choice. You had to be careful, though. He wasn't into hooking up with guys who used the few days at conferences to play with men while away from their wives. You could usually spot them. They had very few ratings on their profiles.

One profile stood out, though. No ratings. Occasionally, you found someone who was newly bi-curious. They could be fun, once you established they weren't stepping out on their spouse.

Silverado3409
61 years old
Professional. Enjoys reading.
Looking for companionship.

Danny hummed as he tapped the screen. Companionship … that could mean anything. Peter had put him in the mindset of hooking up with someone older. A bit of age-gap play.

No ratings, though?

Red flag.

Ah, hell.

Caution to the wind.

<Randyboi289: "Hey.">

<Silverado3409: "Hey.">

<Randyboi289: "You looking for company?">

<Silverado3409: "Are you here for the convention?">

Danny had no problem sleeping with other real estate agents. Most weren't from Victoria anyway. He preferred keeping business and personal separate, but he often made exceptions.

<Randyboi289: "Is that a problem if I am?">

<Silverado3409: "It would be.">

Did that mean the guy was here as an estate agent? Did the guy want to avoid other agents? Danny wasn't sure if he should be honest or not.

<Randyboi289: "Let's go for a drink first. See how it goes.">

<Silverado3409: "You didn't answer my question.">

Might as well tell the truth. If it was a no-go, he could move on.

<Randyboi289: "I am here for the convention.">

Nothing. Danny was about to try the next guy.

<Silverado3409: "I'm just looking to talk.">

Danny sighed. Definitely a newbie bi or gay. An evening talking about someone's burgeoning feelings and desires was not what he was looking for.

It could lead to more later, though.

<Randyboi289: "We can do that over a drink.">

<Silverado3409: "I was looking for something more intimate than that.">

Three bouncing dots.

<Silverado3409: "This is all new to me.">

<Randyboi289: "I'm looking for something more than just

talking. ">

> *<Silverado3409: "I'm willing to head in that direction. ">*

What did that mean? *Head in that direction.* Was the guy willing to have sex or not? This was starting to feel like a waste of time.

> *<Randyboi289: "I'm talking about sex. That's what I want. ">*

A long pause.

> *<Silverado3409: "Okay. Drinks first, though. ">*

> *<Randyboi289: "What's your room number? I'll come pick you up. ">*

> *<Silverado3409: "110. ">*

> *<Randyboi289: "Be there in 5. ">*

He needed to clarify something.

> *<Randyboi289: "One last thing. ">*

> *<Silverado3409: "Yes. ">*

> *<Randyboi289: "Do you have a partner in real life? ">*

> *<Silverado3409: "Widowed. ">*

The guy likely wasn't going to lie about something like that. He could suss him out more over drinks. The talking portion of hooking up with someone was important to him.

> *<Randyboi289: "Be ready for me. ">*

> *<Silverado3409: "Already so ready. ">*

Danny shook his head. This guy better be worth it. He had intended to entertain at least two men today. Walking someone through their first time hadn't been in his plans.

He changed his clothes into something moderately more casual. Still a suit but on the side of more easy-going. He took the elevator to the first floor and found his way to room 110.

He knocked quietly.

The door popped open.

Peter.

Abort!

Abort!

Peter looked as surprised as Danny felt. A flush of red spread from Peter's face down his neck. Straight down to the exposed piece of skin revealed by his open collar.

His cologne drifted past Danny. It gave him shivers under the fierce burning sensation cascading across his skin. Peter looked and smelled damned edible.

But hell no. The guy was Samuel's dad.

How to pull out of this?

"What are you doing here?" Peter asked.

Think quick.

"I asked guest services for your room number. Thought we could go for a drink before dinner. Hope that's all right. You didn't have other plans, did you?"

Peter shook his head and looked up and down the hallway.

"No. Drinks sound good." Peter peered back into his room. "Let me grab my jacket." He was quick about it. Then he shuffled Danny down the hall as he kept looking over his shoulder.

Danny grinned as he walked toward the lounge. He'd totally caught his friend's dad trying to pick up a date with a man for what was probably his first time.

What to do with that.

He considered rolling with it.

They found a quiet spot near some windows overlooking the Vegas strip. Peter was a gin-and-tonic man like him. One had to preserve their figure after all.

"So, you like mystery stories," Danny started.

"Mysteries. Intrigue. Sometimes a bit of historical fiction."

"Mysteries here too. But when I want to bust out, I like to see what the fantasy genre has to offer. Especially the gay stuff."

"Haven't read any of that," Peter said far too quickly.

Danny twirled his drink. The ice tinkled in his glass.

"I was sorry to hear about your wife."

"Thank you. It was a long fight."

"Still doesn't make it any easier."

Peter shook his head. "It sure doesn't."

"How long were you married?"

"Thirty-seven years." Peter took a sip of his drink. "You?"

Danny laughed. "Me. Married? No."

"Never found the right guy?"

"Thought I did." Danny shrugged. "He cheated on me."

"I'm sorry to hear that."

"It is what it is. Not falling for that again."

"You're off relationships?"

"Ones that last longer than one night … yes."

"Don't you get lonely?"

"I enjoy my own company. Plus, I have work. You know how it is. There's always something to do in this business."

Danny pursed his lips as his mind scrambled through a jumble of thoughts. Did he dare? Call Peter out. He was Samuel's dad. Maybe he needed to talk to someone about his sexuality.

He made his decision.

"I was on a gay dating app earlier," Danny said.

Peter blinked at him as he frowned. "Anyone interesting?"

"Yeah. An older guy."

"You're into older men?"

"I have an affinity." Danny smiled and winked at Peter.

Peter groaned and slapped his hand to his forehead, then ran his palm over his hair.

"Jeezus, you're Randyboi289."

"Yes, I am, Silverado3409." Danny reached forward and touched Peter's arm. "Don't worry. I'm not going to hold you to anything. But if you want to talk about it, I'm here."

"I wouldn't know where to start."

"How about the beginning. When did you know?"

"That I'm curious about men?"

"Curious. Sure."

"Since I was a teenager. Then I got married. Put it on the shelf."

"Did it stay on the shelf?"

"The curiosity had a habit of stomping around in my head on occasion."

Danny leaned back in his chair and took a sip of his drink. He set the glass on the table. "So, you were going to do what? Invite some guy back to your room to talk."

"That was the idea."

"You do know what that app is primarily used for, right?"

"I know. Sex."

"Is that something that interests you?"

Peter's face flushed red. It warmed Danny in all the right places. The thought of having Peter's face flush like that for other reasons surfaced. Reasons that involved a bed and sheets.

"Not sure," Peter said.

"You've never imagined being with a man?"

Peter's eyes grew larger. Danny had surprised him by asking such an intimate question. Good. Peter needed to be sure before he hopped back on that app again.

Danny owed Samuel that much. To protect his dad.

"Of course, I have," Peter answered after a moment to swallow hard.

"Does it excite you?"

He was pushing Peter. He knew it. But he didn't want Peter

to end up in a situation that made him panic. A naked man in front of him and the feelings of desire not being there. That was a surefire way to piss off a potential sexual partner. And men could be unpredictable.

Peter looked at his hands. "I started watching gay porn. It definitely excites me."

"That's a good start."

Danny decided he'd made Peter uncomfortable enough. They turned to other topics. Back to favorite books. Favorite music. They both liked classic blues. Hobbies. Peter liked cycling. Danny was primarily a runner. They shared stories of their most lucrative deals.

They'd both done well over the past few years. They delved deeper and Peter spoke about Samuel's addiction and what it had done to the family. And how Peter had grown up with an alcoholic father and how that had made a toxic home life for him as a child.

They turned to a lighter topic. Peter was full of stories about his grandchildren. He loved them dearly. Peter's exuberance for them warmed Danny's heart.

The lounge started to clear. Danny looked at his phone. It was 7:45. Time to head into the banquet hall for dinner. If Peter wanted, Danny hoped they could continue this conversation later.

"We should head over there." Peter rose to his feet, put some cash down on the table, and took a few steps away. He stopped and turned to Danny. "Thank you. Your concern means a lot to me."

"Samuel can owe me." Danny winked at Peter. "Or you could."

"Maybe I'll go easier on you next time we're in negotiations."

"I'd lose respect for you if you did."

"Then we'll have to work something else out." Peter smiled. *Was he flirting again?*

Danny led the way to the banquet hall. It was assigned seating. He ended up at the far end of the large, rectangular configuration of tables with other young agents. Some starting out. Others, like him—their careers on a rocket's trajectory. The group placed him far away from Peter.

Every time he looked toward Peter, Peter was staring at him. A few times, Danny smiled at him. That seemed to fluster Peter. His cutlery crashed onto his plate more than once.

It was endearing, the effect he had on the older man. There was a definite attraction. Peter was off limits, though. Samuel would never forgive him if he found out he'd hooked up with his dad.

After dinner, some of the agents headed back to the lounge. Danny had other ideas. One of the guys at his table had been eyeing him up. Danny had discreetly mentioned his room number in a conversation with their end of the table, complaining about a fictitious hot water problem.

He wasn't surprised when there was a knock on his door half an hour after he arrived back in his room. He was ready. Only wearing a robe. He had an open bottle of wine and two glasses.

Danny swung the door open.

Peter.

Jeezus. What the hell?

"What are you doing here?" Danny asked. Peter looked unsure; brows furrowed over his steel-blue eyes. His silver-touched hair was ruffled as though he'd been running his hands through it.

"Exploring a theory," Peter said.

Peter grabbed Danny's face and kissed him. It was tentative and desperate all rolled into one. Peter's lips crashed against his. Pressed hard—then hesitated. Then crashed again.

The kiss was like a rolling tide.

Danny wasn't sure what to do with his hands. He opted to press them to Peter's chest, to stop him before things got out of control. His cock had swelled with overt interest.

Peter took a step back. "Fuck, I'm sorry … I thought …."

Danny lowered his hands to cover his erection. "No, you're right, Peter. I'm attracted to you. But it's not something we can *explore*."

"My son."

"Amongst other things."

Peter ran his hands through his hair and shook his head. "I'm so lost."

Logical decisions should have been in play, but Danny's grasp on what he should be doing was overridden by what he wanted to do. He wanted to spend more time with Peter.

Danny stepped away from his door. "Come in. Let's talk."

No sooner had Peter made himself comfortable on the sofa than another knock rattled the door. Danny opened it. What should have been his one-nighter was standing there.

"Sorry," Danny said. "Something came up. Raincheck?"

"Tomorrow night?"

"I'll see you around midnight."

The guy cupped Danny's face with one hand. "A kiss to hold me until then?"

Danny leaned forward and took the guy's mouth. He deepened it and added a little tongue, chasing what he hoped to find there.

Nothing.

Not even a twinge from his cock.

Dammit, Peter.

Danny confirmed their meetup time and shut the door. He turned back to Peter. The man was watching him with trepidation. As though he might lose him.

And what the fuck was he supposed to do with that?

Chapter Four | Peter

The feeling was desperation. There was something about Danny that was chasing him. It wasn't just his incredible looks. It was the fear in his eyes about flying. It was the way his breathing had changed when he read to him. It was the concern Danny had for his flailing sexual identity.

It was the way they had talked for hours.

It was the obvious attraction.

He wasn't sure what he'd been thinking. One minute he was sitting in his room. The next minute, he was asking guest services for Danny's room number. Then he was kissing him.

Danny was right to push him away. Peter shouldn't have done it. Attacked him in his doorway without any indication Danny wanted him to. He couldn't understand why Danny had invited him in after that. It was undeniable; he'd interrupted Danny's plans. The wine, the glasses—the kissing the guy at the door. He felt like a foolish old man with more raging hormones than sense.

"I'm so sorry," Peter said. "The kiss …."

"Nonsense. Honest mistake."

So, it was a mistake.

Peter wanted to crawl into a hole. He'd never been so embarrassed. Never. He'd done a lot of stupid things in his life. But this—this took the prize.

"Here. You look like you need this." Danny poured and held out a glass of wine. Peter accepted it and tucked it into his hands. Danny sat beside him on the sofa.

"Walk me through what happened," Danny said.

"I thought we connected."

"We did." Danny took a sip of his wine. "You're not wrong there."

"But you're not looking for a connection. You're only interested in sex."

"You hit it in one."

"And you're friends with Samuel."

"That's the second target hit."

Danny set his hand on Peter's thigh. It was like being touched by a live wire. The tingle shot straight to his cock. His heart thundered in his ears. Danny was speaking but he sounded as though savvierhe was underwater. It was a few seconds before his voice rang back into clarity.

"Peter? Are you all right?"

Peter set his glass down and rose to his feet. "I need to go."

"Whatever you need to do. But I'd prefer if you stayed."

Peter furrowed his brow. "Why?"

Danny shrugged. "I like talking to you."

Peter wasn't sure his lust-addled brain could handle that. Sitting with the young man who had been on his mind ever since that first leg of their flight. He scrubbed his hand through his hair.

For fuck's sake.

Danny was his son's age.

Samuel's friend.

What was he thinking?

He looked at Danny. He was beautiful. An ache spread through his gut knowing Danny was likely nude under that bathrobe.

He should turn and walk out.

Should.

Peter sat back on the sofa and picked up his wine.

"What do you want to talk about?" Peter asked.

"Something simple." Danny lifted his glass. "Let's turn to real estate again."

A recent memory popped into Peter's mind. He smiled. "I have a story you are not going to believe. It involves an ocean view pool, a great dane, and a canoe."

The next hour passed easily. Then two. Then three. It was uncanny how alike they were. Danny was more sophisticated and savvier when it came to real estate, but he had similar hang-ups when it came to speaking to people. He felt as though he had to perform. Become an actor. Peter never would have imagined it. Danny seemed so self-assured.

So confident. So powerful.

So fucking gorgeous.

Peter couldn't take his eyes off Danny. The way his eyes opened and closed with animated expression as he spoke. The little crinkles at the start of his long lashes. The seductive shape of his mouth. How he was quick to smile when Peter said something Danny found amusing.

He was entirely taken with the man.

Peter looked at his phone. It was 5 am. The first speaker was set to take the stage at 9. He couldn't remember the last time he'd stayed up all night talking with someone. He reluctantly removed himself from his place beside Danny on the sofa.

"I'm going to head back to my room," he said. "Enough time for a quick nap and a shower."

Danny lifted his phone. "What time is it?" He rose to his feet. "Damn, that's late. Not sure I'll be able to sleep. Might just head for the nearest coffee urn."

"Youth."

"Hardly. I'm slowing down."

"You have no idea what slowing down looks like."

Danny wandered over to Peter. Facing him, he stepped in close and set his palm on Peter's chest. "I don't see it." He ran his finger down Peter's cheek. "You shouldn't be so hard on yourself."

Peter set his hand on Danny's hip. Danny lingered so close Peter could feel Danny's breath trembling past his lips. The attraction was there. The desire was there.

So close.

Danny moved away. "I'll see you at the first tedious talk."

"I'll be there."

Peter backed toward the door in case Danny changed his mind and let that bathrobe drop to the floor. He'd be on him in a hot second. Danny walked to the bathroom and closed the door.

All the way to the elevator, Peter could barely catch his breath. Danny had ripped his world apart. In its destruction, Peter had found himself. His secret had been set free and a new reality was infusing itself into his bones. He took the elevator to the first floor.

What was supposed to be nap time turned into a lengthy shower. He could crash on his bed after he stroked Danny out of his system. It didn't help. Every time he closed his eyes, Danny drawing a finger down his cheek, close enough to kiss him, invaded his mind.

They'd been close to going further.

Hadn't they?

Peter looked up and down the rows of chairs, searching for the dark, well-groomed hair of the man who had created tornados in his imagination. He spotted him laughing and talking to the woman seated beside him. The chair to the other side of him was empty.

Danny set a program outlining the day's speakers on the free chair.

The move froze Peter in place. Was Danny saving that chair for him or for the guy he'd kissed outside his door last night? Danny looked over his shoulder and spotted Peter.

Danny waved him over.

It sounded like air escaping from his ears as he made his way down to where Danny was seated. A whooshing sound like an airplane taking off.

Sweat collected under the collar of his shirt.

Peter squeezed past a few people and took his seat beside Danny.

Danny nudged him with his elbow.

"Get any sleep?"

"Barely," Peter answered.

"Hard to sleep in a strange bed."

It would have been easier if Danny had been in his arms.

"Yeah. Something like that."

Danny leaned in close to Peter, shoulder to shoulder. He turned his head.

"Something else on your mind," he whispered.

Peter could feel the desire unfurl in his gut. It was ready to respond. He swallowed. Sweat broke out on his temples. Why now? Why tease him in public?

He shifted in his seat as his cock swelled. He set the program of today's speakers that had been sitting on his chair on his lap.

"A lot of things," he whispered back.

"Anything I can help you with?"

Jeezus.

Peter closed his eyes and willed his body to slow down. He was reading sexual innuendo into a conversation that might be perfectly innocent.

Danny's knee came to rest against Peter's.

"Maybe I could work it out," Danny said, then rubbed his leg against Peter's. "Tell me what you need, and I might have changed my mind about being there for you."

Peter almost groaned.

He scanned their surroundings to see if anyone was paying attention to the way Danny was pressed against him. Two rows in front of them, he spotted Ryan; his best friend, Maxwell's, son. It had slipped his mind that Ryan would likely be there. It reminded him he had a son in his thirties.

Like Danny.

Danny was easily twenty-five years younger than him.

What the hell was he thinking?

Peter brushed his knuckles against the hand Danny had placed on his thigh close to Peter. He was thinking that age had nothing to do with the connection they had made.

"I'm really not interested in hearing this speaker," Peter said.

"Are you absolutely sure?"

"Never surer."

"Then let's go." Danny rose from his seat and followed Peter as he led them up the center aisle to the door into the concourse. Once they arrived there, Peter wasn't sure what to do next.

"Are we going to one of our rooms?" Peter asked.

"That's the general idea, yeah."

"Yours?"

"Sure."

Danny started to walk toward the elevator, but Peter stopped him by grabbing Danny's elbow. "Just so we're clear … I've never done this before." Peter didn't want Danny to get any ideas that he was taking someone in any way experienced back to his room.

"I know. I'll be gentle. I promise." Danny stroked Peter's arm. "Maybe start with a massage. See how you like it. Go from there if you're feeling comfortable."

He should have expected it—that Danny wouldn't push him. During their conversation the night before, Peter ascertained that Danny was a kind, caring, and generous person.

He was perfect.

Everything about him was perfect.

He was ready to trust him with this.

Danny's room looked different than the night before. The daylight flooded through the curtains. Peter hadn't considered that—that every wrinkle and age spot would be on display. The elegant young man removing his clothes across the room might find them repugnant.

"Don't be shy." Danny walked toward him. Glorious in his nudity. Every muscle toned to perfection. Broad, powerful shoulders and chest. Cut abs. Trim hips.

And his cock.

Peter's heart rabbited in his chest. Not even fully hard, it was thick and long amongst groomed black hair, resting on a set of perfect pink balls.

Danny's hands came to rest on Peter's chest, then started undoing the buttons of Peter's shirt. The shirt slipped off Peter's shoulders onto the floor at his feet.

Peter groaned as Danny ran his fingers through the abundant grey hair on his chest.

"God, you're sexy," Danny whispered.

"Not too old for you?"

Danny stepped closer. "You're perfect."

Peter wrapped his arms around Danny's waist as Danny took his mouth. The kiss was warm and loving, as though he meant something special to Danny.

Maybe he did.

He sunk into it. Enjoying the give and take of two men coming together in a moment of understanding and enlightenment. Danny's hands moved to Peter's belt.

Danny unlatched it, pulled fast, and slung the leather length onto the floor. He moved back and sat on the edge of the bed. "I want to watch you take the rest off."

The nerves started in Peter's veins. He ignored them. He trusted Danny and knew his lust would win out over timidity. He removed his shoes, pants, underwear, and socks.

Danny leaned back on the bed and tipped his head to one side, studying Peter.

"I knew you were gorgeous under that suit," he said and rose to his feet. "Find a comfy place on the bed, facedown. I have some massage oil in my travel bag."

Peter did as he was asked. He stretched out on the bed and pulled a pillow under his head. It felt strange lying there in the nude, waiting as Danny fussed around in the bathroom.

The bed sagged as Danny climbed on. He straddled Peter's hips.

A rush of desire flowed from Peter's toes all the way to his lips as Danny's ass settled on his. Along his tailbone, Danny's balls and semi-hard cock came to rest.

Danny started at the back of Peter's neck and along his shoulders. His hands were broad and strong. Firm, capable fingers. The hands of a man.

"Just relax. This doesn't have to go anywhere. Just enjoy it for what it is. All right?"

"Mm." That's as much as Peter could manage.

As Danny's fingers dug and caressed, a sense of calm descended on Peter. His shoulders, down his spine, his ribs, back up to his shoulders—his arms. Danny shifted and came to rest on Peter's thighs. The tip of Danny's hard cock pressed against the crease of Peter's ass.

Danny used his thumbs to loosen Peter's glutes. He spilled more oil into his hands and grabbed handfuls of Peter's flesh. With each pass, Danny worked his fingers lower. He shuffled backward.

Peter gasped as Danny pried his ass cheeks open and exposed his hole to the air. Danny released him. Then did it again. And again—and again. Peter had to fight to relax his muscles and let Danny take him on the ride he had started him on.

Danny's thumbs crept closer and closer until one brushed across Peter's tight opening. Peter groaned and ground his hips into the bedding. He'd never been touched there by anyone. His body's reaction was an unexpected response. He wanted more. So much more.

"Did you like that?" Danny asked.

"Yes."

"Do you trust me?"

"Yes."

Danny shifted down further, then slid one knee between Peter's legs and encouraged him to open them. Peter could feel Danny moving around. Danny's arms came to rest on his thighs.

Hot breath gusted past his ass cheeks. Danny gripped his hips.

A single kiss on the crease of his ass.

"Is this all right?"

"Yes."

Danny's hands were back on his ass. Peter clenched the bedding in tight fists. His flesh was pried apart. After several tries, Danny was satisfied. Danny's thumbs held him open wide.

"Still good?"

"God, yes."

Peter moaned as Danny's hot tongue licked his pinched hole. Danny dug deeper, burying his face in between the mounds. Danny groaned as he worked his tongue. Licking swaths. Prodding. Circling the tight ring. Devouring Peter with his lips. Slick and wet. The rough texture of Danny's trim beard added to the sensations firing off between the cheeks of Peter's ass.

Peter released a long breath and relaxed. He was rewarded as Danny's tongue pushed a short way into his body. He nearly blissed out. Never had he felt anything like it.

"That's it," Danny whispered against his skin. "Let me in."

It took all of Peter's willpower not to grind his cock into the bedding.

Each thrust of Danny's tongue was accompanied by Danny undulating his body and moaning. Peter could feel the shift in the mattress between his legs. This was turning Danny on. That surprised him for some reason. He imagined being between Danny's thighs and eating his ass.

His cock pulsed.

Yeah, okay, I get it.

Time passed but Danny didn't relent. With each lick and prod of his tongue, Peter's arousal grew. His cock was close to releasing the incredible tension building in it.

Danny moved from Peter's ass and massaged his thighs. He rose to his knees.

"You can turn over when you're ready."

Peter's heart skipped through a little offbeat. Danny moved aside as Peter rolled over. Peter's cock was rock hard and weeping. Danny's face was shiny from the massage oil.

"Do you want to cum?" Danny asked.

It was an odd question. How would he not after that?

Peter nodded his head.

Danny palmed Peter's cock. "Can I suck you off?"

Another question that should have an obvious answer. Peter ran his fingers along Danny's arm. "I need your hot mouth on me again."

Danny grinned then leaned forward and licked a long line up Peter's tight cock. It was agonizingly insufficient ... and Danny knew it.

"More," Peter whispered.

"Like this?" Danny's lips encased Peter's cock, tongue pressed to the length, and lowered his head until Peter's cockhead touched the back of his throat.

It was almost enough to make Peter cum.

Peter ran his hands through Danny's hair.

"Yeah, like that."

Danny wet Peter's cock as he ascended. Then slid back down. Peter kept his hands in Danny's hair as he bobbed up and down. Danny's fist clenched his shaft. His other hand played with Peter's balls. Peter arched his back and clenched and released his ass in time to Danny's motion.

Fuck.

Danny looked incredible down there between his legs.

Peter gripped a handful of Danny's hair, grunted, and came hard.

They'd missed lunch. Ryan had texted him and asked where he was. Right now, though, Peter was simply content to watch

Danny sleep. He looked so serene.

He nearly reached out and touched his perfect lips.

Peter tucked his arm further under his head instead.

God, he was young.

There was a maturity about him, though. And the connection they'd made wasn't something to be ignored. They were like two arrows that had been loosed from opposite ends of the world and were inexplicably drawn to occupy the same bullseye. They had talked for hours again.

Danny had insisted he didn't need to cum.

They talked more about Peter's dysfunctional and abusive childhood. About Danny's amazing parents and his somewhat picturesque life growing up. The boyfriends Danny had during high school and college. About Dominique and how he still plagued Danny's psyche. How being cheated on had colored Danny's view on relationships. How much Peter still missed his wife.

Then Danny had fallen asleep beside him.

Hours passed. Peter had slept for a while as well. Their night of staying up until 5 am had wiped them both out. They'd started off tangled together. He'd fallen asleep holding Danny.

Peter couldn't stand it any longer. He stroked Danny's fingers. His thick lashes fluttered, and his eyes emerged. Flecks of gold and brown watched him.

Danny smiled at him.

"Hi."

"You're beautiful when you sleep."

Danny laughed softly. "Thanks?"

Peter stroked Danny's hair.

"What have we done?"

"Got ourselves in over our heads, I'm afraid."

"I feel so close to you."

Danny frowned. "Peter … you know we can't do this again."

It was a spear to his heart. Peter couldn't imagine walking away from this man. He wanted to wrap Danny up in his arms and protect him from the world for the rest of his life.

The revelation shocked him.

"I don't think I can live with that," he said.

Danny touched Peter's face and cupped his jaw. "In a different world, I wouldn't be going anywhere. But we live in this world. One with your son Samuel in it."

Danny was right. Peter knew it. But he still wanted to fight for more time with Danny.

"Tonight, and tomorrow night? Can we have that at least?"

Danny shut his eyes and sighed. He opened them again.

"Honestly, that scares me a little."

"Why?"

"I like you."

"Why is that a problem?"

Danny rose onto one elbow. "It just is." He threw off the covers and swung his legs out of bed. "I'm going to have a shower. You're welcome to join me."

Peter rolled onto his back and stared at the ceiling as Danny left the bed, and the water in the shower started up. He scrambled out of bed. This might be the final time he would be caressed and kissed by the incredible young man who was dangerously close to stealing his heart.

He didn't want to waste a single second being away from him.

He stepped into the shower with Danny. He was met by warm, wet hands on his face, and pulled into a long, lingering kiss. Danny released his lips and hovered above them.

"What the hell have you done to me?" Danny said.

"I don't know what to do with what I'm feeling."

"What are we going to do?"

"I don't know."

"Fuck." Danny placed his forehead against Peter's. "I don't want you to leave."

"Then, I won't."

"We can't stay here all night. It's already 7. We have to make an appearance at dinner."

"I'm all yours until then."

"Then, that's it for us," Danny said. "We can't continue this."

Peter's heart and mind were at odds.

He simply nodded.

Danny frowned at the floor of the shower, then smiled at Peter.

"I better make the most of it," he said.

He moved in for another kiss. This one was more desperate. Peter wrapped his arms around Danny. His skin was smooth, and his hands were destined to glide down to Danny's ass. He cupped and caressed the firm globes. Danny moaned into his mouth.

Peter pulled his lips away from Danny's.

"It's your turn," Peter whispered then sank to his knees.

Danny's hard, thick cock came into view. Peter rubbed his cheek along it and just savored the moment. He lifted Danny's balls and kissed each one. Danny ran his hand through Peter's hair.

Peter licked his lips as he stared at Danny's cockhead. He knew that if they weren't in the shower, he'd be able to see it glistening with desire. He licked the tip, then wrapped his lips around it. It felt incredible against his tongue. He dragged a circle around the ridge of Danny's cock, then dove on. Danny grunted, tipped his head back, and clung to a clump of Peter's hair.

It was something he had only dreamed of. Having another man's cock in his mouth. The feel of it approaching his throat was more glorious than he had ever imagined. He worked to increase his saliva. He lifted his head away and got his tongue ready to dive back down.

He took Danny deeper this time. It was both exhilarating and frightening. He coughed as Danny's cock hit the back of his throat. Danny moved his hand to the side of Peter's face.

"You're doing fine without going that deep."

Peter slurped and released.

"I want to. I want to feel you filling my throat."

Danny furrowed his brow. "You sure?"

Peter nodded.

"Move back," Danny said. "Let me put my hands on the tiles above you."

Peter shuffled back until his toes touched the far edge of the shower enclosure. He looked up at Danny and opened his mouth. He placed his hands behind his back and clasped his fingers.

Danny looked down at him. "You are so fucking sexy."

Without using his hands, Danny fed Peter his cock. He started slow to let Peter adjust his breathing. He increased his pace. Peter shut his eyes and relaxed. With each withdrawal, he took a breath. Danny went deeper. It set off a bout of coughing.

It was intoxicating.

He wanted more.

Peter raised his hands and cupped Danny's ass to encourage him. Once Danny had the pace set Peter was aiming for, Peter lowered one hand, gripped his hard cock, and pumped it.

Danny swore, groaned, and grunted as he watched Peter pleasuring himself.

A swift gentle thrust.

Peter sputtered and gagged as Danny spilled down his throat.

He whimpered in objection when Danny withdrew from his mouth. Danny dropped to his knees, water spilling over his head. Water dripped off his lips. He took over stroking Peter's cock.

Peter placed his hands back behind him, gripped his ankles, and raised his hips. His cock was on fire with longing. He desired release more than his next breath.

Danny tugged fast and hard until Peter saw stars and erupted. He pumped into Danny's hand until he had milked out every drop.

Peter lowered his hips. He felt as if he was going to pass out. He placed his hand on the tiled wall and tried his best to catch his breath. His difficulty must have been evident.

Danny gripped his elbow. "Let me help you up. Your legs must nearly be asleep."

It took a couple of tries, but Peter eventually made it back onto his feet. It was embarrassing. He had struggled to get his legs to cooperate. Danny had been a gentleman about it.

Danny wrapped one arm around Peter's waist: his other hand on his face.

"You surprised me. Wanting that," he said and kissed Peter. His tongue searched out every crevice of Peter's mouth. His cheeks, the roof of his mouth—under his tongue.

Peter gasped as Danny released him. "It felt good. I can still taste you."

"I like to share in that … to taste myself on you."

That made Peter shiver with a new wave of desire.

Danny brushed his hand through Peter's hair. "We need to get cleaned up and down to dinner before Ryan starts texting you again. Next thing you know, Samuel is going to be looped in."

Samuel.

Peter looked at Danny. What on earth did this young man see in him? Danny could have anyone. Anyone at all. Even straight men probably appreciated his looks and physique.

He ran his hand down Danny's chest through the black offering of hair. Back up again. He wanted to imprint the feel and warmth of him in his mind. Memorize each breath Danny took. His steady heartbeat. Danny's hand as it caressed Peter's back. Peter closed his eyes.

If he concentrated, he could encapsulate everything he was feeling.

This was it.

They wouldn't be sharing another moment like this.

Peter found his spot in the banquet hall and took a seat. Danny was at the opposite end. He was glad of it. He couldn't get the man off his mind. He needed time to think. They had been adamant they couldn't continue this. Peter groaned and stared at his place setting.

There were still two nights left before they flew home. Despite what they'd decided, Peter wanted to spend the rest of that time in Danny's arms. If he could convince him.

They had mixed up the estate agents' seating this time. Younger agents alternated with older ones. Even so, he was a bit surprised when Ryan sat next to him.

"Hey," Ryan said. "What happened to you at lunch today?"

"Got tired. Climbed into bed for a while. Lost track of time."

Not a complete lie.

"I didn't see you at any of the speaker events either," Ryan pushed on.

"Wasn't really into it. I had work to do."

"Have you been down to the casino floor?"

"No."

Ryan unwrapped his cutlery and set it to one side of his place. He laughed and nudged Peter. "Not sure why you came down here if you're in your room working. You could have stayed home."

Peter laughed.

He was so glad he hadn't stayed home.

If he had, he wouldn't have made an intimate connection with the beautiful, caring, warm young man at the opposite end of the banquet table.

Peter sighed.

"I'll try to have a bit more fun."

"I'll hold you to that."

"You talk to Samuel?" Peter asked.

"Yeah. Told him you were missing in action."

"No need to do that. I'm fine."

Samuel would have been worried about him. Meanwhile, he had been in bed with one of Samuel's good friends. It was a breach of trust. He frowned.

What had he gotten himself into?

Peter glanced down the length of the table at Danny. He was animated as he spoke to the agents around him. Holding the floor. They were probably lapping up everything he had to say. Very few agents came along who were as successful as Danny. He was a wonder.

And off limits.

For Samuel's sake. Any plans of pursuing Danny and

convincing him to spend the next two nights together were off the table. He needed to clear the man from his mind.

Peter realized he had fallen silent. He turned back to Ryan. "You get anything useful out of these speaker events?"

"The importance of a good photographer and what to look for in their work."

"Crucial. People go by their guts before they decide to view a property. It's like a book cover. If the pictures don't grab them, it's a no-go."

"One guy covered negotiation skills."

"Danny would be the guy to talk to about that."

Ryan raised his eyebrows. "You follow his sales?"

"Who doesn't? We all have something to learn from him. Even us old-timers."

A twinge of desire coiled inside him. Danny had taught him so much in the short time they were together in bed. And out of bed. An image of Danny in the shower towering above him, his cock riding his tongue. Pumping—thrusting. The feel of him filling his throat.

His breathing sped up.

Ryan touched Peter's arm.

"Are you all right?"

There was genuine concern there. The type of concern you'd have for an elder. An *are you having a heart attack or a stroke* kind of concern. An *are you about to drop dead*? kind of concern.

Peter scowled. At sixty-one, he still felt young most days. Others—everything hurt. He needed to nap at least once a day. He had trouble staying awake past 9 pm.

He had no business longing for someone like Danny. They were right to end it. He would do his best to avoid being in Danny's presence for the next two days.

It would hurt too much to be near him.

Peter joined the line of people queued up for the long table of food. There was a vast selection. Pastas, salads, scalloped potatoes, chicken, rib-eye beef, roast carrots, cabbage rolls … it was more choice than Peter needed. His appetite wasn't what it used to be.

A hand touched the center of his back. He turned his head. It was Danny.

He'd cut in line.

"What looks good besides you?" Danny whispered.

"Everything *on the table*." Peter wasn't about to play into any kind of sexual banter. Their time together was done. They needed to head back to their respective corners.

"I can't stop thinking about you," Danny pressed on.

Peter's breath caught.

Why? Why was Danny doing this? They couldn't continue this. He thought they'd agreed they needed to stop. They'd had their fun. Entertained themselves with a scandalous affair.

Peter closed his eyes.

God, it was so much more than that.

"Please don't," Peter whispered over his shoulder.

"Don't what?"

"Don't do this. We can't. I don't want to."

His chest nearly collapsed when he felt Danny move away from behind him.

A feeling of loss cascaded through him.

Chapter Five | Danny

The rest of the convention crawled by. Danny just wanted to go home. Attempt to heal his injured heart. His intense yearning for Peter had come out of nowhere. By some grace of God, Dominque had decided against attending the convention. Danny was able to be alone in his thoughts.

He had even turned away his one-night stand guy last night.

Danny leaned back and crossed his arms, only half-listening to the speaker droning on about self-promotion. Something he was already skilled in. He could've done a better job of speaking.

Tears filled his eyes. He swiped the heel of his hand across them before the tears spilled down his cheeks. Peter had been firm in their decision.

Don't do this. We can't. I don't want to.

The words kept bouncing around in his head. It had been him not Peter who initiated it—the fact they couldn't continue seeing each other. Now, he was regretting it.

He'd made a bid in the banquet room, hoping Peter would cave.

"Hey, buddy."

Danny sniffed hard and looked to his right. "Hey, Ryan."

"Didn't expect you to be in here. You have promotion nailed down."

"I'm hiding."

"From what?"

"It's a who."

"Hookup gone wrong?"

"Something like that." Danny blew out a long breath. "I let

my emotions get involved."

"That's not like you."

"I know but he crawled under my skin somehow."

"You gonna see him again?"

"No. He was very clear about that."

"Conference is almost over. Long distance sucks anyway."

Danny pressed his lips closed. He wouldn't be telling Ryan his heart had been stolen by someone local to Victoria. The flight back home was going to be awkward enough. Fate better not deal him a low blow and place him beside Peter again in the plane.

This was the last speaker of the conference. He planned to head down to the casino after this. Drown his sorrows by losing a ton of money at poker.

"I'm peacing out." Ryan stood and patted Danny's shoulder.

"I'll come with you. Drinks?"

"Sounds like a good start to the evening."

They crowded into the throng of agents in the lounge and found two spots at the bar. Gin and tonic. Two—then three. The pain started to ease.

"So … what was so special about this guy?" Ryan asked.

No … please … don't.

Danny stared at the bar top. He didn't want to dig around in his heart. Name all the emotions he was battling. Replay the time he and Peter had spent together. His chest ached.

The distress was too intense to contain.

"He was everything I didn't know I needed."

"He didn't feel the same way?"

Danny looked up at Ryan. "That's the thing. He felt it too."

Ryan frowned. "I'm sorry, man. That really sucks."

So much more than sucks.

It was going to take him months to recover. Now that he'd

shared a bit of what he was feeling, he wanted to put the turmoil out of his mind.

"I don't want to talk about it anymore."

"Respect. I'll drop it."

Danny drained his glass and set it on the bar top. "Want to head down to the casino?"

"You read my mind."

Twenty-thousand dollars later Danny had succeeded in making himself feel worse. He wanted to wallow in it. Remind himself why he shouldn't let his emotions come into play.

He collected what chips he had left and looked around for another table to lose at. He wasn't even trying to win. He was a shark at poker, but he'd deliberately been making bad decisions.

He surveyed the last table he hadn't played yet. There was an empty seat.

His chest rose and fell with strained effort.

Peter occupied the seat next to it.

Danny couldn't stop himself. Just to sit near him. Maybe he could try again. He slipped into the empty chair. Peter looked over at him and scowled.

Danny let out a small, quiet whine when Peter threw his cards down on the table and stormed off across the casino floor.

It really was over.

He folded his arms on the edge of the table and placed his forehead on them. He felt as if he was going to be sick. Maybe that's what it felt like to have your soul slowly torn to shreds.

Ryan sat beside him and placed his hand on Danny's shoulder.

"Buddy ... what the hell? Are you all right?"

Danny lifted his head. "I think I've had too much to drink." It was only coming up to 7 pm but Danny felt as though he'd been there all night. The world had become sluggish.

Ryan rose to his feet. "Let's get you back to your room." He helped Danny to his feet and walked with him out through the casino doors and across the foyer to the elevators.

Danny struggled with his key card at his hotel room door. Finally open, he turned back to Ryan. "Thanks." He patted Ryan's arm. "Can I ask you for another favor?"

"Yeah. Sure."

"Can you bring me up some dinner? I'm going to nap, then get some work done. I'm not really in the mood to see people."

"Hookup guy again?"

Danny nodded. "It's destroying me."

"That's rough. Can you not try again?"

"No." Danny shook his head. "He wants nothing to do with me."

"Try to take it easy. We'll be back home tomorrow. You can start to heal there."

"Do my best. Thanks again."

Danny closed his door. Going home wasn't going to fix things. He'd end up seeing Peter on the regular. They were bound to work together on occasion. His clients always came first. He couldn't exactly ignore Peter's listings. They'd be spending time on the phone together.

He made good on the need for a nap. He was awoken by Ryan knocking on the door, a plate heaped with food in hand. It was more than he could possibly eat. He thanked Ryan and headed for the dining table by one of the windows. It was dark out. The twinkling, flashing lights should have made him feel better, but they just reminded him of what happened in Vegas on this trip.

God.

Danny leaned on the table and placed his head in his hand. He was so tied up in knots on the inside, he wasn't sure he could eat anything.

He abandoned food for work. He had a couple of new listings his assistants were working on that had come in while he was away. He needed to look them over. The pictures were already done. He'd need to sign the paperwork when he returned.

He immersed himself in contracts and listing descriptions.

Danny looked at his phone. 10 pm. Peter would likely be back in his hotel room. Ryan's words played in his mind. *Can you not try again?*

His face flushed as he considered taking one last shot. He ran his hand through his hair and gripped a handful. This was insane. Even considering it.

Still—his legs propelled him to his door and down to the first floor.

Room 110.

He knocked quietly in case Peter was already in bed.

There was noise on the other side of the door. And then nothing. Peter had probably looked through the peephole and was considering whether to open the door.

It opened slowly.

"Danny ... what are you doing here?"

"I had to see you."

Peter leaned against the doorframe. He looked adorable. Grey hair, all messy from the effects of a pillow. Boxer shorts that showed off his legs. An open dress shirt that must have been thrown on for the sake of modesty. And his eyes. Steel-edged blue watching him with apprehension.

"We talked about this," Peter said. "We can't continue

seeing each other."

Danny gripped the front of Peter's shirt. "I can't do it. I can't breathe."

Peter frowned.

Danny sighed and tugged on the shirt in his grasp. "Please don't turn me away." Just one more night. That's all he needed. A final night in Peter's arms.

"What do you want exactly?" Peter asked.

"I just need you to hold me."

Peter's brow dipped, then he stepped back and swung the door open.

Air sank from Danny's chest to his belly. He felt as though he was about to pass out. Another chance ... he was being given another chance. He was quick to enter the room.

The door closed and Peter trapped Danny against it. Chest to chest. Thighs touching. Arms to either side of Danny's shoulders.

"You've undone me," Peter said and stroked Danny's face.

"I want to be around to put you back together."

Peter moved away. Stepped back across the room. "How?"

"Let's not worry about that right now." Danny wandered up to Peter and took him in his arms. "Right now, I just need to feel your embrace."

Peter was fast to kiss him. A hand around the back of Danny's neck to keep up the pressure to increase the intensity. Danny's hands were frantic. He shed the shirt from Peter's body.

He ran his thumbs under the elastic waistband of Peter's boxers.

His mind pumped the brakes.

Slow.

The dance needed to slow down. It needed to last.

He wanted to remember every second of it.

He gripped Peter's ass, pulled him close, and swayed back and forth as if there was music playing. Peter's fingers went to work unbuttoning and removing Danny's clothes.

Danny stepped out of and discarded everything. He placed his hands on Peter's hips and lowered his boxers to his ankles—slow and easy.

Peter kicked them aside.

Danny, nude, kneeled before Peter and kissed his abs. He would do anything for this man. Peter just needed to name it … and he'd do it.

He looked up at him.

He blinked as he watched Peter.

"Tell me what *you* want," Danny said.

"I want to feel your skin against mine." Peter touched Danny's shoulder and indicated he should rise back to his feet. He took Danny's hand and led him to the bed.

"I want to hold you," Peter said.

They lay on the bed, their heads on a single pillow, chest to chest—hip to hip. Danny swung his leg onto Peter's hip and pulled him closer with his heel. Their erections brushed together.

Peter cupped Danny's face and kissed him. His lips were soft and warm—like coming home after a long trek through snow and ice. Danny gripped Peter's neck. He rocked his hips in a slow rhythm. Their cocks prodded against each other and the soft flesh of their bellies. Danny hauled Peter closer by placing his hand on Peter's hip and tugging.

He rolled Peter onto his back, their lips found each other again—and again.

His thrusting became more desperate. Peter parted his legs and Danny sank between them with his thighs. He wrapped his arms around Peter and clung to him. He couldn't imagine ever letting him go. He buried his face in the space between Peter's ear and shoulder, along his soft neck. Panting and sighing, Danny undulated his hips. Peter's hips rose to meet him.

Their hard cocks ground against each other. Danny lifted himself on one arm, spat a few times into his free hand, then coated their cocks in slickness. Peter clung to Danny's waist and drew Danny back to him. Back to being layered beneath Danny. Back to his lips.

The sensuous kiss was long and intense.

Danny headed to his safe space against Peter's neck. He kissed, licked, and nuzzled Peter's skin as he continued the loving tip and retreat of his body. His ass clenched and released, each thrust bringing them both higher. He took a moment to look down into Peter's face.

Peter had his eyes closed; mouth open … the sweetest damned sounds drifting from it. Occasionally, he would close it and grunt softly. Danny kissed Peter's cheek and buried his face back in the warm and humid space behind Peter's ear.

He could live in this moment forever. Peter wrapped his legs around Danny's thighs and drew him even closer. He dug his fingers into the flesh of Danny's back.

Peter's nails dragged across his skin so hard Danny knew for sure, he'd been marked. Peter bucked beneath him and filled the space between them. Danny's cock was set loose to slide through the sudden lack of friction. He kissed Peter's neck as he jerked and added to the slick pool.

His brain was addled. The lust and emotion still strong. The release—the connection. The longing. He'd never felt closer to anyone in his life.

He couldn't stop it.

The feelings washed through his heart and soul—and

erupted.

"I love you," he whispered.

Peter struggled beneath him. He grabbed Danny's face and pried Danny away from him. He rolled Danny off him and onto his back. He towered over him. Peter looked angry.

Danny's heart sank.

Peter shook Danny's shoulders.

"Don't you dare joke about something like that."

Danny scowled. "I wasn't joking."

Peter flopped down on the bed beside him. His chest climbed and fell, exhausted. He was taking a moment to think. That was encouraging at least.

"It's not possible," Peter said. "What on earth do you see in me?"

"I see an incredible man I can see myself with … long term."

"We've known each other for what … three days?"

"I don't know what to tell you. You stole my heart. I've never felt like this before."

Peter rose on one elbow and stared down at Danny. "We're not possible. We discussed this."

"Then let's discuss it again. With new information. My love for you isn't going anywhere."

Peter's facial features softened. "You're serious."

"I am."

Peter closed his eyes, tipped his head back, and sighed.

"What the fuck are we going to do?" Peter said.

"Try. We need to try."

"How?"

"Carefully. We can't let anyone know," Danny said.

"That's a given. Samuel and Ryan would never understand."

Danny nodded.

Understatement of the year.

For once, Danny was glad of the cramped quarters in a row of airline seats. It meant he was able to keep his knee against Peter's for the duration of their flight. They'd switched seats to be beside each other under the premise of being amid working on a deal together.

No one had batted an eye.

They shared a cab even though they lived at different ends of town. Peter in Fernwood and Danny in Oak Bay. They covertly held hands for the whole trip. The ache to kiss Peter before he climbed from the cab was strong. He resisted. Danny slid down in the cab's lonely back seat.

He leaned his head back and grinned at the ceiling.

He was in love.

It was early in the morning, but Danny couldn't contain his excitement anymore. His mom would likely be up anyway. He selected her number and waited for her to pick up.

"Danny! What a nice surprise."

His mom sounded chipper. She was a naturally positive person. It had been fun growing up with her. She always had sound advice and the ability to make you feel good about yourself.

"Got back from a real estate conference last night."

"How was it?"

Danny wasn't sure how he was going to fill his mom in on all the details. He wanted to tell her everything. Get her opinion.

"I met someone," he said.

"A man?"

Danny laughed. "Yes, a man. An incredible man."

Even though his parents had accepted he was gay, they still had this weird fantasy that he was going to find a girl someday who would make him reconsider.

"Is he a real estate agent?"

"Yes, and he's based out of Victoria ... so no long-distance nonsense."

"That's good." His mom fell silent—then, "Tell me about him."

"He's amazing. Intelligent, funny, sophisticated. We have so much in common. We talked for hours and hours. When we were away from each other—it was agony."

"Sounds serious."

"It is, Mom." Danny stroked the sheets. "I'm in love."

"Love? So soon?"

"It was intense—the time we spent together. We packed so much into the hours we spent with each other. It was like dating someone for much longer."

"But love, Danny."

"I've never felt this way before, Mom. Not even with Dominique. He broke my heart, but he never had every bit of it in the first place. It's different with Peter."

"Peter. That's his name?"

"Yeah. Peter Anderson."

His Mom didn't respond, but he could hear her breathing. "I knew a Peter Anderson," she said finally. "Back in high school. He was two years ahead of me."

Danny's heart ramped up its pace. He knew Peter had grown up in Victoria, but he'd never asked Peter what high school he went to. What neighborhood he had lived in.

Danny cleared his throat. "Mom ... promise me you won't freak out."

"You're scaring me. What is it?"

Danny sighed. "It might be the same guy."

His mom didn't answer.

"Mom?"

"Why, Danny? Why would you do that?"

"Do what, Mom?"

"Get mixed up with someone your father's age. When you told us you were gay, we accepted it. Hoped you'd think better of it, but if not, we thought you might find a nice boy to settle down with. Someone your own age. Someone you could have children with."

"Mom … you know I don't want children."

"A mother can dream."

His mom murmured to someone in the room. Probably his dad. Luckily, his dad hadn't grown up in Victoria. It would be strange if Peter had been a high school friend of his.

His dad sighed through the phone.

"What are you doing, Danny?

"Enjoying being in love with a man who makes me happy."

"He's on the verge of being an old man like me. Another four years and I'll be retiring. I'll be considered a senior. So will he. Why would you want to tie yourself to a sinking ship?"

"He's not sinking. He's virile and strong." Danny switched the phone to his other hand. "And I don't care that he's older. I've promised him I'll be there with him—through it all."

"How can you make a promise like that? You barely know him."

"I can't explain it, Dad. We were destined. My heart decided for me. I had no say. When I was away from him … when I thought it was over between us—I couldn't breathe. I longed for him from my very soul. I want to be wrapped up in his arms forever. I love him, Dad."

His dad grunted.

"We'll need to meet him."

"Give us a while, please. We need to get used to the idea of being together as a couple. I promise, though … I want you to meet him. You'll see what I see."

"He makes you happy."

"Giddy. I've never been swept away like this."

His dad grunted. "Okay. I'll hold judgment until I meet him, though."

"I wouldn't expect anything less."

His mom said his name. She had taken the phone back.

"Be careful," she said.

"Always am."

"That's not what I meant. I want you to promise me you'll protect your heart."

"How am I supposed to do that?"

"Hold a little back until you're sure."

"Mom, I'm all in already. I'm sure of what we have. Trust me."

"I don't want you to get hurt."

"I'll survive if it goes sideways. Won't need to, though."

Pause.

"I'm glad you're so happy."

"Thank you, Mom."

"I'm burning bacon … have to go."

"Right. Yeah … okay. Love you, Mom."

"You too."

Danny ended the call. It had gone as well as he had expected. A little hesitation by his parents, but in the end, they were happy he was happy.

He and Peter had agreed to talk on the phone later tonight. He had a lot to tell him. About his parents; about his day once he made his way through it. He needed to know if Peter had known his mother in high school. Peter would have been a senior when his mom was still a junior. When it was laid out like that, the age difference between him and Peter felt strange.

He rolled over in bed. He didn't care. He loved the man. His age had nothing to do with it. Yeah, it added to Peter's sophistication and his looks. The silver-grey hair was sexy on him.

But it was the person inside he'd fallen in love with.

The age of the packaging was more than secondary. It was inconsequential.

Chapter Six | Peter

Peter stopped walking to take in the view of the ocean. Its ancient vastness reminded him that whatever joy was happening in his life, he wouldn't be around forever to enjoy it. Love didn't come around often. And over these past few days, he'd been blessed with receiving it.

He tugged his coat tighter around him. The wind had picked up. He hadn't seen Danny since they returned to Victoria. Their schedules kept conflicting. The wait was agonizing. They'd been like a couple of teenagers, talking to each other on the phone late into the night.

Last night, he'd fallen asleep to the sound of Danny's voice.

They made a date for Saturday. Dinner and drinks. There was no issue with them being seen together in public. There was an easy excuse of them having a work meeting.

Peter looked out to sea. The wind whipped past his face.

It was one week since Peter had spoken with Danny at Samuel's recovery birthday.

So much had happened since then.

It had happened so fast. Or had it? They'd spent countless hours talking to each other in Vegas. Time had blurred they were so immersed in each other. And little of it had been small talk. They'd opened up to each other. Spoken of insecurities and hopes. History and regrets.

And the sex.

Goddamn. The sex had been incredible.

Then those three mind-shattering words.

I love you.

Danny had been so adamant he wasn't looking for a

relationship that the admission of love had stunned Peter. It had stunned Danny too. Danny understanding how he felt and why had taken a few tries. Danny had talked. Peter had listened. Danny needed to work it through.

It was stunning. Listening to a young man come to an incredible realization. Discovering that his heart had found a place to nest. That he needed another human being—desperately.

And it was for him. The love.

A tear ran down Peter's cheek. He hoped he was worthy.

His phone buzzed in his pocket. It was a number he knew well.

"Danny."

"Hey, Peter. I have some clients here who are interested in your Humber Road property."

"I'm not in my office right now but if they want to set up a viewing, I can do that."

"They're motivated to move quick."

"I'll make a call and see how soon I can get them in. Later today shouldn't be a problem. My clients are over in Europe for the winter. I just have to check with the caretaker."

"Perfect."

A wash of desire flooded through Peter with that word. Danny had called him *perfect* when he was assuring Peter he was desirable. During their last night in Vegas, Danny had kissed and nuzzled every square inch of his body. He'd seen it all. And still loved him.

They'd almost missed their flight.

"I'll give you a call back with a time."

"Thanks, Peter."

The call disconnected. No, *I love you*. No, *I can't wait to see you*. It was strange to talk to Danny and not have it be personal and warm.

Peter called the clients' caretaker. 2 pm would be the best time for him. He texted Danny with the time. He smiled and added a heart to the message.

He received a set of red lips in return.

A scroll through their text messages would give them away in a heartbeat. Loving words of affection amongst business texts. They were taking chances and they knew it.

The danger factor was exhilarating.

Peter pulled up outside the property at 1:50. Danny was already there with his clients. They *were* motivated. He approached Danny's car and Danny rolled down his window. They chatted like casual colleagues for a few minutes to pass the time. The whole time, Peter wanted to lean in and haul Danny to him and take control of his lips. Breathe in the scent of him.

They both had the acting portion of their personalities down pat.

Peter stepped away from Danny's door. "I think it's safe to head on in." He waited for Danny's clients to join them, then led the way along the walkway. "I just need to talk to the caretaker. Verify you are who you say you are. Formality."

"Whatever you need to do." Danny gave Peter his space as Peter rang the doorbell. After a quick conversation with the caretaker, Peter stepped back. "I'll be in my car. Give me a holler if you have any questions about the property."

Danny reached out and shook Peter's hand. "Thanks."

They lingered for a moment, their skin in full contact. It was hard to let go. Danny smiled at him, then led his clients into the house.

Peter headed back to his car. He pulled out his phone. He almost sent Danny a text message to share how agonizing that had been. But Danny would be in the middle of his tour of the property. He'd be showing them all the rooms, the exquisite back garden, and the view of the ocean.

He had every confidence that Danny would sell them that house.

He set his phone in the cup holder.

There would be time to text him later. Maybe while they were working out the sales figure, they could sneak in a few personal comments. Thirty minutes later, his phone rang.

It was Danny.

"My clients are ready to make an offer."

"What are they thinking for numbers?"

"3.8 million."

"Respectable. Write it up and I'll present it to my clients. I think you might have a sale."

Silence.

"I'm in a back room," Danny said. "Alone."

Peter released a sigh. "Shaking your hand … it was agonizing to let go."

"I wanted to pull you in for a kiss."

"Not sure how I'm going to survive dinner on Saturday without being able to touch you."

"Good conversation will help ease that ache," Danny said. "Can I stay at your place after?"

Peter's heart bloomed with anticipation. An entire night with Danny was more than he had hoped for. Making love, falling asleep, and waking up with him was like a dream.

He grinned. "I don't know. Do you snore?"

"You know I don't."

"Then I guess that's all right."

Danny laughed. The rolling baritone of his voice carried through the phone. Making Danny laugh more often was a quest Peter was prepared to embark on. The sound fed his soul.

"I'll call you after I send that offer to you," Danny said.

"Looking forward to it."

"Love you."

"You're the most precious thing to me." Peter hadn't told Danny he loved him yet. He wanted to be sure. His heart was pulling hard in that direction, but he wasn't there yet. The memory of his wife was still fresh. He'd loved her. But what he had with Danny was different—more intense.

"Okay. Bye."

"Bye."

Peter looked at the time. He was having Samuel and his wife over for dinner at 5 pm. They had hired a babysitter for the night. Dinner, drinks and maybe a board game. It would be a fun night. They hadn't had a night like that in a while. He'd been occupied by his mourning.

Danny had pulled him the remaining way out of that grief.

There were groceries he needed to pick up. He was going to do something unexpected and cook for a change. He enjoyed cooking. He'd enjoy it more if Danny was with him.

He was making Dry-Rubbed Chicken Breast with Honey Mustard Potatoes and Kale Salad. A quick turn through the grocery store and he was ready to follow one of his late wife's recipes.

A bit of office work first. But that was quick.

He started with the potatoes. Cut them up, then coated them in olive oil, a bit of salt and pepper, and placed them in the hot oven on a baking sheet. He mixed the spices he would need. Added a bit of oil and made a paste. He massaged the chicken with it and set it aside.

Peter sat at the kitchen island for a few minutes and thought about Danny. He pulled out his phone and opened his text messages. Danny had sent him a string of hearts.

<Peter: "How's your evening? I'm having Samuel over.">

<Danny: "Work. Had a ton of listings come in. Sometimes too much promotion backfires.">

<Peter: "That's a great problem to have.">

<Danny: "Can I send some of these listings your way? I'm overloaded.">

<Peter: "I'm happy to take them on. I have room for a listing or two.">

<Danny: "Perfect.">

That word again. *Perfect.*

<Peter: "Got to get back to cooking. I'll call you tonight after Samuel leaves.">

<Danny: "Okay. Looking forward to it.">

<Peter: "XOXO">

<Danny: "Kisses.">

Peter got his head back in the game. The salad. Green onions, dill, and kale. A mayonnaise, honey, sherry, and grainy mustard dressing. All mixed together in a large bowl.

The doorbell rang. Peter washed his hands, walked to the front entry, and let his son and his wife in. They'd dressed up for the occasion. A night out was a *night out* when you were a parent. He remembered it well. He had loved raising his son but sometimes you needed a break.

He was happy to provide that break for Samuel.

"I'm just putting the chicken on now," Peter said as he lifted down two wine glasses. One for him. One for Samuel's wife. For Samuel, he had bought some dealcoholized beer.

"Should be another fifteen minutes until this is done," he added. "Help yourself to something to drink. There's some 0% beer in the fridge for you, Samuel."

"Awesome, Dad. Thanks." Samuel went to the fridge.

Grabbed the wine and beer. He poured a glass of Chardonnay for Peter and Laurel and cracked open his beer.

Peter lay the three chicken breasts in the pan layered with hot oil. It sizzled as he set each piece down. "So, Danny and I might have a deal on the Humber Road property."

A warmth grew in his gut.

Danny and I had rolled off his tongue as though the words were meant to be used together.

"That's quite the sale," Laurel said. "Love that area of Victoria. We sometimes drive through the Uplands neighborhood just to look at the grand houses."

"Danny talks about wanting to buy a house in Uplands someday," Samuel said. "Wouldn't put it past him to do it. The guy is on fire."

"He's talking about starting his own agency," Peter added.

"You've been talking to him?" Samuel asked.

"We spent some time together at the conference."

"How was it?"

Peter knew Samuel was talking about the conference, but he so badly wanted to tell his son how he had spent those few days with the most incredible man.

A man who was clinging to his heart.

"Spent most of the time working. Made some good connections, though."

Lies.

The only connection he had made was with Danny.

"Other Canadian agents?"

"American too. I have people from the States interested in some of the properties north of the border. Investment homes. Summer homes. Somewhere to get away to."

"Must be nice," Laurel said. "We can barely afford the mortgage on our little townhouse."

Peter flipped the chicken and then removed the potatoes from the oven. He mixed them in with the salad. "There are a lot of people out there with money. And I'm grateful for it."

He looked around his kitchen. He'd had it renovated two years ago. It was gorgeous. His wife had let him have carte blanche. He'd exercised his designer muscles, drawing from the many houses he'd toured over the years. It was very French château'esque.

It had been the last room in the house to be renovated before his wife died.

He looked at his son. Samuel had been devastated by the loss of his mother.

Danny was lucky that way. Both of his parents were alive and healthy. And they'd accepted the fact he was gay with a *Yes, we know*. They had an amazing relationship. Danny's parents were Peter's age. In fact, his mother was younger than him. It made Peter uncomfortable.

He divided the salad onto dinner plates and added the chicken to each.

"Grab a plate," Peter said. "We'll eat in the dining room."

They all wandered to the table, found a spot, and dug in. There was silence for a few minutes as the first bites were enjoyed. There was something on Peter's mind.

He set his knife and fork down.

"How would you feel about your dad dating someone younger?"

Samuel raised his head and set his fork down. "How much younger? Like forty-five?"

Peter shook his head. "No. Younger than that."

Samuel's eyebrows rose. "Like a woman in her 20s?"

"No." Peter laughed. "That would be a bit extreme."

"Someone my age?" Samuel leaned back and crossed his

arms. "Kind of sick, Dad."

Peter felt as though he'd been shoved in the chest. If his son wouldn't even accept the age gap, how would he accept that it was a man … and that the man his dad longed for was a good friend.

It might be too long a road to acceptance.

"It was just a thought," Peter said.

"I'm sure you can find a suitable woman your age if you're ready to start dating."

Peter wanted to holler that he didn't want a woman. That would knock his son right off his feet. That his dad was gay. He'd come to terms with it. He'd been living a lie with his wife. All those thoughts. His secret. It had been coming from his very depths. He was gay.

He couldn't contain its existence.

"I'm gay," Peter whispered.

Samuel's cutlery clattered onto his plate. "What?" He shoved his chair back and rose to his feet. "You're what? You didn't honestly just say you're gay?"

Peter sighed. "I did … I am."

Samuel sank back into his chair. "When did this come about? You were married to Mom for thirty-seven years. So what? You were just pretending?"

"I hadn't fully processed what I was feeling. Who I am."

"But it was there. You knew it was there. The attraction to men."

Peter nodded. "Yes."

"So, you used Mom as a beard."

Peter glared at Samuel. "I never used your mother. I loved her."

"Loved her … but you were gay the whole time."

"Samuel, for all those years … I wasn't sure."

Laurel took a sip of her wine and then set her glass down. "That's not unusual. Men your age didn't have the gay examples out there like the kids today do."

"I wish I had," Peter replied. "Would have saved me some time."

"Time for what?" Samuel leaned back from the table and jammed his hand into his hair. "Jeezus, Dad. Does that mean you want to date *men* my age? That's just creepy." He lowered his hand. "Wait. Are you dating someone already?"

Peter wanted to tell Samuel and Laurel the truth. That he was close to falling in love with an exquisite young man. A man who could change the course of his life.

"Not yet."

"Please don't," Samuel said. "That would make for some uncomfortable family meals. I don't want to end up someday with a stepdad my age or younger."

Peter hadn't even thought that far ahead. Where was his relationship with Danny going? Realistically. Danny had said he wanted to be with him long-term. What did that mean?

"You're not upset that I'm gay."

Samuel scowled. "Not upset … just surprised." He chased a potato around his plate. "Are you sure? You're not just imagining things because of your grieving process."

Peter shook his head. "I've tested the theory."

Samuel slammed his fork down. "Jeez, Dad. I don't want to know about that."

"I'm sorry."

"I need to wrap my head around this." Samuel closed his eyes. "My dad is sleeping with men." He opened his eyes. "Mom would be horrified."

"She's not here anymore."

"What if she was? You didn't ever go behind her back, did

you?"

It hurt that Samuel would even ask him that. Of course, he hadn't. His marriage had been sacred to him. He took marriage vows seriously. He'd committed himself to her.

"Absolutely not. I only came to terms with my sexuality over the past week."

Samuel's eyes widened. "The conference? You hooked up at the real estate conference?"

Peter sighed and nodded.

"Another agent?" Samuel pushed on.

"I'd rather not say."

Samuel coughed out an expulsion of air. "You did. Oh, my god … you did." He slammed his hand on the table. "How old was he?"

"Old enough."

"Fuck … Dad. I can't accept this. You can't be cradle-robbing. What the hell has gotten into you?"

That's all Samuel was getting *out* of him. Peter had walked halfway down the long road to acceptance. The last half was quicksand. It would swallow Peter and destroy his relationship with his son. As it was, Samuel was in absolute disbelief. He refused to push Samuel any further.

He needed to talk to Danny.

They couldn't do this.

Saturday.

Saturday night, he'd break it to him.

Chapter Seven | Danny

Danny and Peter had been on the phone on and off over several hours—for business. They spent some of their time feeling each other out on the selling price of the Humber Road property.

An offer had been sent and now they were in negotiations. Both were intent on getting the best deal for their client. They had started at 3.8 million and the seller had counter-offered with 4.1 million. Danny was trying to work a deal based on the fact the roof needed to be replaced along with several gas fireplaces. And it was possible the heritage home needed work done to the foundation. Danny's clients had countered the counteroffer with 3.95 million dependent on what was found during a full inspection of the home. It would slow down negotiations for a few days.

They'd switched to texting. Some interactions between real estate agents needed to remain private. It allowed them to discuss details before sending official documents.

<Danny: "My client will deduct any potential costs from their offer.">

<Peter: "Fair enough. I think my clients are amenable to that.">

<Danny: "Realistically, it'll end up around 3.9.">

<Peter: "My clients are expecting that. They know there are repairs to be done.">

<Danny: "Then we're headed in the right direction.">

<Peter: "We should have a deal soon.">

Danny tapped his finger on the edge of his phone. One of his assistants usually went through his phone once a week to make sure he hadn't forgotten anything. He'd kept it out of her hands for days now. Peter knew. They'd discussed getting burner phones. The idea seemed extreme.

For now, he was going to play *keep away* with his phone.

<Danny: *"I'm excited about dinner tonight."*>

<Peter: *"Yeah, we have lots to talk about."*>

Danny furrowed his brow. That sounded serious. His love for Peter had grown while they were apart. Thursday night's phone call lasted for hours and reinforced what he was feeling. He'd never fit that well with someone in his life. It would devastate him if Peter pulled away.

<Danny: *"Are you planning on backing out on us?"*>

<Peter: *"We'll talk later."*>

Danny slipped his phone back into his suit pocket. He was going to try to not dwell on how cold Peter sounded over text. He turned back to his clients.

"We should hear back from the inspection company about an inspection date before the end of the day. They're usually quick about getting back to me."

His clients were a gay couple with plans to open a B&B in the home. There were zoning bylaw hoops to jump through before they could start their business, but Danny had assured them the property lent itself to such a venture and would receive approval from the city.

His mind turned back to Peter and his stomach twisted. His nerves were firing off alarm bells. What had changed? Peter had Samuel over for dinner the night before. Perhaps that's when the change of heart happened. Peter had made an excuse of being too tired to talk on the phone that same night. Last night. That should have been enough warning that something was up.

He said his goodbyes and left his clients' house. He slid into the driver's seat of his car and sat there, staring out the windshield. He retrieved his phone.

<Danny: "Are you planning on breaking up with me? I don't want to go for dinner with you tonight if that's what you're planning.">

<Peter: "There are things we need to talk about.">

<Danny: "What things? Please don't spring anything bad on me tonight.">

The pause went on for almost a minute.

<Peter: "I told Samuel some stuff.">

<Danny: "What kind of stuff?">

<Peter: "That I wanted to date someone younger. Someone his age.">

<Danny: "What did he think of that?">

<Peter: "He hated the idea. Honestly, he was repulsed by it.">

<Danny: "Does that make a difference? We connected. Age has nothing to do with it.">

<Peter: "He's my son. It matters what he thinks.">

What did one say to that? Of course, it mattered what Samuel thought. But maybe he'd make an exception if Peter found someone he was in love with.

Danny frowned.

Peter wasn't there yet. He was close to love. Danny could feel it through the phone when they spoke on Thursday night. It was on the tip of Peter's tongue.

<Danny: "I know it matters. But it matters what you think and feel, too.">

<Peter: "You already know what I think and feel.">

<Danny: "That you want to be with me.">

<Peter: "To my very core.">

Pause.

<Peter: "But Samuel.">

There it was—black and white.

Peter *was* planning to put an end to their relationship.

Danny scrubbed his hand along his jawline. There had to be a way to fix this. Maybe if they discussed everything somewhere private, Danny could talk Peter out of ending things.

<Danny: "Instead of dinner tonight. Come to my house.">

He waited for Peter to respond.

<Peter: "Okay. One last night.">

This *was* the end. Danny's chest tightened. He wanted to scream and fill his car with the sounds of anguish. He choked back the tears. It was going to tear him apart, but he needed what Peter had offered … one more night. Then he would let his heart fall to pieces. The dreams he'd had of spending the next twenty years with Peter would be left strewn about and destroyed.

<Danny: "One night. That's all I'm asking for.">

<Peter: "I'll be there at 9.">

<Danny: "Perfect.">

Danny started his car and backed out of the driveway. The drive home was quiet. He'd switched off the radio. He needed to roll through his emotions uninterrupted.

Tears filled his eyes as he drove. There was something so strong between them, it was undeniable. Being separated from Peter … one might as well tear straight into his heart and strangle it. He clung to the steering wheel as a wave of panic washed through him. One night. He needed much more than a night. He needed a lifetime. He wanted a lifetime.

He slammed his hand on the steering wheel.

"Fuck!"

Back home, Danny went straight to his bedroom and changed his clothes. Black slacks and a black and gold striped shirt, open at the collar. The black color suited his mood.

He lay on his bed, set his phone down on the bed, and curled into a ball. The onslaught of sobbing and tears wracked his body. He rocked and swore and soaked his pillowcase.

This couldn't be happening.

The agony was unbearable.

Danny cried himself out and eventually fell asleep, his face on the damp bedding. He awoke to the sound of the doorbell. He snatched up his phone and looked at the time. 9:32.

It wasn't like Peter to be late.

Maybe Peter had toyed with the idea of not showing up.

Danny straightened out his clothes and jogged down the stairs to the front door. He waited a few seconds, held his breath, and opened the door.

He nearly crumpled to his knees at the sight of Peter.

Peter had been crying.

His face was mottled. His eyes were puffy and rimmed with dark pink.

"Babe," Danny whispered and reached for Peter. He guided him inside, closed the door, and folded Peter into his arms. "We're going to figure this out."

"I don't want to let you go."

"I know. I can't imagine life without you either." Danny took Peter's hand and led him into the living room. They took spots on the sofa tight against each other. Their hands remained linked.

"I don't want to do this," Peter said.

"Do what? Discard my love for you?" Danny was going to be brutal. Peter was planning to throw away all the love he had for him. Peter needed to be reminded of that.

Peter furrowed his brow. "You mean it, don't you? When you say you're in love with me."

"Babe, I couldn't be surer." Danny stroked Peter's cheek. "You mean everything to me."

Peter looked down at their linked hands. "I don't know what to do with that."

"Cherish it. Explore it. Fill every single day with it."

"I want to." Peter reached up and cupped Danny's face. He leaned forward and kissed him. Then placed his forehead against Danny's and filled the space between them with his warm breath.

"Then do," Danny said. "Do it. Let me love you."

"What about Samuel?"

"He doesn't have to know yet. We can keep this between us."

"Yet."

"If we sink deep enough with each other, we'll have to tell him eventually."

Peter sat back. "That terrifies me."

"This is your life. You have every right to be happy despite what Samuel might think."

"I believe that … in theory."

Danny squeezed Peter's hand. "Then take a leap and believe in us."

Peter heaved out a breath. "I came here tonight to end things. For many reasons. You told me you were thinking long-term. I don't know what that would look like for us."

Danny decided to take a leap himself.

"It would look like two men in love."

Peter sighed and studied Danny's eyes. "Exactly how old *are* you?"

"Just turned thirty-four."

Peter rocked his head to one side and groaned. "I'm twenty-seven years older than you. When I'm in my eighties, you'll be in your early fifties. Too young to be tied down to an old man."

"That's my decision." Dany gripped Peter's thigh. "I don't see your age. I love *you*."

"You'll end up being my caregiver."

Danny hadn't thought about that. That Peter might become infirm someday. It didn't matter, though. He loved the man. He'd be honored to be the one who was there to care for him.

"Then so be it," Danny replied.

"You say that now."

"And I'll keep saying it."

"You'd break my heart if you abandoned me."

Danny moved closer. He stroked Peter's shoulder, then clung to it. "I'm not going anywhere. I'll never go anywhere without you. I can make you that promise right here—right now."

Peter's gaze wandered from Danny's eyes to his lips, to their joined hands, and back to Danny's eyes. "That's a huge promise."

"One I will live by."

Peter nodded slowly. "Okay."

Danny straightened. "Does that mean disaster averted?"

"We don't tell Samuel yet."

"My lips are sealed."

Peter grinned. "Not too sealed, I hope."

Danny laughed while releasing a sigh of relief. "I'm sure I can find a way to fit you in."

Peter leaned in and kissed Danny. Danny deepened the kiss, crushing his lips against Peter's. He let the love pour out through them. He wanted to fill Peter with it.

Danny pushed Peter backward onto the sofa cushions. Peter lay flat on his back, his hand around the back of Danny's neck to keep their lips joined. Danny shifted and Peter dropped his legs open to accommodate Danny's body. Danny lowered himself to be chest to chest with Peter.

Danny thrust slow and easy with his hips to build the tension as unhurried as he could manage. This was meaningful. They weren't in Vegas anymore. The thrill of hooking up amongst their peers was gone. They were home now. He wondered if the full desire would still be there.

Peter groaned into his mouth and met Danny's thrusts with his own.

Their cocks swelled between them.

The desire *was* there.

Danny grasped Peter's face and turned it away so he could access Peter's neck. He set a row of kisses along Peter's bristled jawline, then tucked up behind his ear. He licked and kissed and nuzzled the soft skin there, then headed down his neck. He pulled Peter's shirt aside and focused on the skin at the base of Peter's neck. He set his mouth to it and sucked hard. Unless Peter had his shirt off, the mark wouldn't be visible. But he'd know it was there. They both would.

Peter groaned and ran his hands up Danny's back, then held Danny's head in place.

"You're going to leave a mark," he said.

Danny released Peter's flesh. "I know." He located the reddening skin and set his mouth back to it. Peter wrapped his legs around Danny's hips and tugged him close.

"I'm yours," Peter whispered. "I'm all yours."

Those words meant the world to Danny. It was a step away from Peter saying his heart was his. Even the words Peter *had* spoken weren't a commitment to be taken lightly.

He would treat Peter with tenderness with every loving ounce of his soul.

Mine.

Danny lifted his head. Satisfied with the purple mark he'd left on Peter's skin, he climbed away from Peter. He stood and held out his hand. "Let's take this to the bedroom."

Peter held Danny's hand and followed him upstairs to the sleek, sophisticated bedroom that Danny rarely shared with anyone. He usually used the guest room with *visitors*.

"Undress for me," Danny said and sat on the edge of the bed.

Peter's fingers danced along his shirt's button, undoing them. Then shed his shirt. His pants and socks were next. Peter moved slowly as he lifted his underwear over his hard cock and shoved them down his legs and onto the floor. He stood with his hands at his sides.

Danny hummed. Peter's body was toned. He'd taken care of himself. He was furry. The only parts of his body that weren't covered in hair were the area along his ribcage and his upper arms.

"Turn."

Peter turned around. No hair on his back. A light dusting on his ass. Danny closed his eyes and took himself back to the time he had spent with his face between those globes of muscle, teasing Peter's hole into submission. Feeling it fall open for him.

"Come to me."

Peter faced Danny and walked toward him. Danny tugged Peter close until he was able to place a kiss on each of Peter's hips. His cheek brushed against Peter's straining cock.

Peter quivered as Danny licked a line along Peter's shaft.

"Jack it for me."

Peter did as he was told. He gripped his cock and began stroking it. After a few moments, Danny touched Peter's hand to still it. He sucked on the cap of Peter's cockhead and ran his tongue through the slit. Peter moaned and thrust his cock into his hand.

Danny sat back. "Keep doing that."

It was a sight; watching Peter pleasure himself. His eyes closed. His mouth open—moaning, his hand increasing in speed. Danny's heart thudded in his chest as he waited.

You could see it in Peter's change in stance and the stilling of his hips. Danny closed his mouth over Peter's cockhead and took the first shot of cum to the top of his mouth. The rest on his tongue. He didn't swallow. He savored. This was a gift from the man he loved.

Spent, Peter dropped to his knees. Danny leaned forward and shared what he had collected. Peter was hungry for it. His tongue flew around inside Danny's mouth.

Danny left a soft kiss on Peter's lips. He gripped Peter's chin as he looked at him.

"You did well," he said.

"I'll do anything you ask."

Danny's eyebrows rose. He hadn't expected Peter to be so willing. They would leave *anything* for another day. Tonight, he wanted to focus on love. Not love and submission.

Danny unbuttoned his shirt. He tapped Peter's shoulder to get him to move out of the way so he could remove his clothes. He stood and discarded everything. Peter shuffled up the bed until his head was on one of the pillows. Danny met him there and sealed their lips together.

Peter felt good beneath him. Solid and strong. He knew Peter wouldn't always feel that way. The day would come when he would have to be more careful. The thought took up space in his mind for less than a second. This was now. And right now, the man he loved was in his arms.

Open-mouthed, sloppy kissing escalated his desire. Every taste, every swipe of Peter's tongue, every slippery wet lip— all of it. Peter wrapped his legs around Danny's thighs. His heels hooked around them, refusing to let Danny go. Peter's hands cruised up and down Danny's back, then grabbed his ass. He set the pace of Danny's thrusting hips.

Peter arched his back and threw his head back as Danny scraped his teeth across Peter's chin. The sound of the bristles filled Danny with surges of deep-seated lust. Peter was all man. A craving he'd embraced his entire life. He increased the thrusting of his hips. Peter was hard again.

Danny squeezed his eyes shut, tight. "Babe, I'm going to …." The words didn't escape soon enough. He flooded the space between them. He rested his forehead on Peter's cheek.

Peter stilled.

Peter wrapped his arms around Danny's body and hugged him. Maybe Peter had changed his mind again. One last hug before he abandoned him.

"I love you too," Peter said.

Danny rose on one elbow and looked down at Peter. "You're sure?"

"There have been few things I've been sure about in my life. This is one of them."

Danny smiled and gave Peter a quick kiss.

"Not post-coital pillow talk," Danny said.

Peter laughed. "No. I mean it. I love you."

"And you're not going anywhere."

"I'm staying by your side through whatever storm is going to befall us."

Danny rolled off Peter and flopped down on the pillow next

to his. "Best day of my life."

Peter turned to face him. He stroked his finger along Danny's temple. "Mine too."

"You mean that?" Danny flicked his gaze to Peter's eyes.

Peter laughed. "Close second to the day we adopted Samuel."

"Fair enough." Danny smiled.

"I told him I'm gay." Peter moved his thumb across Danny's lower lip.

This was news. In all the hours they'd spent talking, Peter had never indicated he'd made a decision about his sexuality. "You are?"

"Pretty sure. I've never been attracted to women. Lusted over a lot of men over the years, though. I wasn't keen to label what I was feeling, but I wanted to say something to Samuel that he would understand. I landed on gay."

Danny rolled and supported his head on his hand. "That's a big deal."

"No. What *we have* is a big deal."

"You never felt this way about your wife?"

"We were high school sweethearts. I did what I thought I was supposed to. Meet a girl. Go to university. Start a career. Marry her. Start a family."

"Cookie cutter."

Peter nodded. "What we have is different. I'm in this for me—and you. We aren't going through the motions to fit someone else's idea of what we should be doing."

"Including Samuel."

Peter furrowed his brow. "Yeah. I can't control how he's going to react."

"He will still love you."

"Maybe. Might not ever talk to me again, though."

"Don't say that. You don't know that for sure."

Peter rolled onto his back. "We'll know when we know."

"It's not something we have to worry about for now."

Peter smiled. "No. Right now, I'm enjoying you, your company, and your love."

Danny put his hand on Peter's chest and played with the curly grey hairs. "That's plenty for now. It's our little secret. Let's revel in that." He smiled. "A private love."

They quietly enjoyed the moment. Their love was real. Realized—and spoken.

Peter broke the silence. "I enjoyed that … you telling me what to do."

Danny had been wondering if Peter would bring it up. He was glad he had. Eventually, it would need to be talked about. They hadn't discussed sexual preferences in all their time talking. This was one of his kinks—submission. It was important to him.

"You responded well," Danny said. "It's meant to be a release. You're under a lot of stress in everyday life."

"Is it something you do often … take command?"

"With some people. They have to be into it."

Danny could practically hear the wheels turning in Peter's mind. Peter was frantically rubbing one of his fingers across his thumb. He spun a ring around on his finger a few times.

"I would do it again," Peter said.

Danny pressed a kiss to Peter's cheek. "I'm glad."

Chapter Eight | Peter

Peter wasn't sure what he'd agreed to. He had enjoyed Danny taking control and telling him what he wanted from him. Danny was right. It was a relief for someone else to be in charge.

Especially someone he loved.

A knock on his office door made him surface from his thoughts. One of his assistants, Carol, the woman in charge of his bookkeeping popped her head in.

"Do you have a minute?" Carol asked.

Peter leaned back in his chair. "Sure. Come on in."

Carol had a handful of paper in her hand. She closed the door behind her. "First I want to say, no judgment." She set the papers on Peter's desk. "I just want to make sure it's not a mistake."

Peter sighed. He had a pretty good idea what this was about.

"I'm looking over your phone bill," Carol started. "And there have been some long calls between you and Danny Miller. They last until early in the morning."

It was starting. Their private love was about to creep into their public life. They knew it would happen as soon as those first phone bills came through.

Peter had hoped they would have more time.

He was slow to answer.

"The long, late-night calls, Peter," Carol said.

"Yes, and yes, Carol."

"You and Danny."

"Since the real estate conference."

Carol lifted the papers and put one hand on her hip. "Is it serious?"

"Very."

"Does anyone else know?"

"No … and I don't want you telling anyone for now. We're not ready."

Carol studied him. "I didn't know you were gay."

"I'm what Danny calls a late bloomer."

Carol crossed her arms. "He's your son's age, isn't he?"

That was going to be the sticking point for most people. Not that they were two real estate agents in a gay relationship. It was going to be the age gap that threw people off.

"It's not an issue for us."

"People are going to talk," Carol said.

"Let them."

"It might harm your business. Both of you."

It had been a lengthy topic of conversation between him and Danny, about what this was going to do to their businesses when word got out. They might lose clients. Some agents might avoid working with them. They had clung to each other. Fear and resolve had brought them to tears, as they'd agreed to ride out the potential upheaval together.

They were in love.

"We know," Peter replied. "We're ready for whatever the world has to throw at us."

"Are you … are you really? It's not just you, you know. Other people rely on you both to put a roof over their heads— to feed their children."

Peter scowled. Of course, they had considered it. They both had enough money saved up to pay their staff for almost six months while they looked for new jobs or weathered the storm.

"You'll all be well cared for, I promise."

Carol didn't look convinced. She was scowling.

"What's happening with the Humber Road property?"

"We're still in negotiations."

"You and Danny?"

He knew where Carol was headed. "I'll ask Darren to take over for me."

"I'll send him in to see you."

"Thanks, Carol."

When the door shut, Peter folded his arms on his desk a set his forehead on them. Carol was right. They couldn't be on opposite ends of a deal. They were a couple now.

Peter rolled that around in his mouth. A couple.

Partners.

They'd discussed it and decided to skip over the boyfriend label. They were in love. Their relationship required a suitable title.

Partners.

He pulled the word around him like a warm coat. It fit. He had connected with someone who made sense to him. He'd never felt that with his wife. They'd been a couple, but they had never felt like partners. He had allowed himself to be towed around by her desires.

He'd always been afraid to express his opinions with her. Afraid she might leave him. And then what? He'd be left alone to confront his secret. He hadn't been ready.

Now he was.

And Danny was by his side. Truly by his side. Last Saturday night was still like a dream. Saturday night—Sunday morning, they hadn't left each other's sides. They'd talked. They'd slept curled around each other. They'd showered together. They'd cooked breakfast.

They'd made love.

Again—and again.

Peter had barely managed to pull himself out of there on Sunday night.

He wanted to be back there. Back in Danny's arms.

Back to where his world made sense.

They had a plan to go running after work tonight. The snow was gone. The streets were dry. They were having a bit of a warmer spell. Cycling was more Peter's speed, but he wasn't averse to running. It was usually restricted to his treadmill, though. The cold air was going to be a shock.

A soft knock and Darren swung open the door. "Carol said you needed to see me."

This would be person number two.

"Sit down," Peter said. "Close the door." He waited for Darren to close the door and settle in a chair in front of his desk. "I need you to take over the Humber Road negotiations."

Darren's brow furrowed. "That's *your* baby."

"I'll give you half the commission."

"That's generous … but why?"

"Conflict of interest."

"With whom? Danny?"

Peter nodded. "We're involved."

"Involved?" Darren gripped the edge of the desk. "Like involved—involved?"

"We got to know each other at the conference. Things progressed from there." Peter leaned back in his chair. He tapped the desktop as Darren stared at him, mouth open. "I'd prefer if you kept this to yourself for now. Not sure how it's going to affect the business."

"I'm not comfortable with this."

"With taking over the negotiations or my relationship with

Danny?"

Darren shook his head. "See, now that just sounds wrong. Your *relationship with Danny*. You were what … almost thirty when he was born? And I didn't know you were into men."

"I'm gay, Darren. And Danny's age doesn't come into play when it's just us."

Darren shuffled forward on his chair and leaned on Peter's desk. "I've known you for almost twenty years, Peter, and I think you're making a big mistake. When you're thinking about retirement, he'll be at the height of his career. He's not going to have time for you."

It was a fear—that Danny would tire of him. As he aged, Danny might think better of his decision to saddle himself with an old man. That he would withdraw from him. Leave him.

Peter's chest tensed with doubt. He caught himself. He needed to believe. When Danny spoke of their love, he used words like *forever* and *no matter how things change*.

"I trust Danny," he replied finally.

"It's about more than trust."

"I know. We have more."

Darren released a long sigh and scooted back in his chair. "Just looking out for you."

"I appreciate it."

Darren rose to his feet and headed for the door. "Send me the files. I'll close this deal."

"Don't let Danny bully you too hard."

Darren laughed. "Just my luck that you'd hook up with a bulldog."

Peter smirked as Darren closed the door. He was proud of Danny. Proud to be with a man as accomplished as Danny. Proud to call him his partner.

He lifted his phone from his desk.

<Peter: "Miss you.">

<Danny: "Miss you too.">

<Peter: "Carol and Darren know. My phone bill came in.">

<Danny: "It was always going to happen eventually.">

<Peter: "Darren is taking over Humber Road.">

<Danny: "Makes sense. I was going to bow out myself.">

Of course, Danny would be on top of something like that. He had a stellar reputation to maintain. A reputation that was likely to be hit hard. They were putting their lives and their livelihoods on the line. They both felt it was worth it to take that chance. It was always possible people wouldn't bat an eye. That's what they were hoping for.

Peter hadn't seen Danny in days, they'd both been so busy. He needed to be back with him. To see his smile. To get lost in his intense expressive eyes. To feel his arms around him.

<Peter: "I need to see you.">

<Danny: "We're running tonight.">

<Peter: "And after?">

<Danny: "Shower back at my place and dinner?">

<Peter: "That sounds amazing. Do you need me to pick up anything?">

<Danny: "Nah. I love cooking. I always have plenty of options on hand.">

Peter chuckled and smiled. *Danny loves cooking.* There were still things he was discovering about him. So many layers to become familiar with. Enough to last a lifetime.

<Peter: "I didn't know you liked cooking. So do I.">

<Danny: "We can cook together anytime you want.">

<Peter: "Is that an open invitation?">

<Danny: "I'd love to have you over as often as possible.">

<Peter: "I'm going to hold you to that.">

<Danny: "You can hold me anytime. I love your arms. I love you.">

<Peter: "Love you too. See you at 6 on Dallas Road at the sundial.">

<Danny: "I'll be there."> *<heart emoji>*

The rest of the day was tiresome. The client Peter spent the afternoon with had been searching for their dream property for three months. Nothing was good enough.

They had wrapped up the fourth viewing of the day. The properties Peter had shown them were too small. Too big. Too dark. Too bright. The list went on and on.

He was running out of patience.

Actual running was going to be just what he needed.

Peter arrived at the sundial right on time. Danny was waiting for him. He looked delectable in his running gear. Black leggings, white sweatshirt, black beanie, and gloves. He was jogging in place to keep warm. When he saw Peter, a smile lit up Danny's face.

Peter couldn't stop himself. He wrapped Danny up in his arms and held him. There were very few people around on a chilly, dark evening. Danny clung to Peter and kissed his cheek.

"Hey, babe," Danny whispered in his ear. "You feel good."

Peter rocked Danny back and forth in his arms. He never wanted to let go. But it was cold, and they needed to start running or freeze to death. He released Danny.

He stepped back and looked Danny up and down. "And you *look* good."

"It's dark." Danny draped his arms around Peter's neck. "But I'll take the compliment." He ran his gloved hands across Peter's beanie. "Can I kiss you?"

Peter peered around. There were a couple of people

walking dogs. He decided he didn't care. He cupped the back of Danny's head and captured his mouth. The kiss was short but intense.

"Wow … yum." Danny stroked the grey hair at Peter's temples.

"You're incredible."

"You're full of compliments tonight."

"What can I say … I'm smitten."

"Just smitten?" Danny smiled, stepped away, and jogged in place. Steam gusted from his mouth. His nose and lips were red from the cold.

Peter motioned for them to start running. "More than smitten. Word on the street is I've fallen in love with this amazing guy."

Danny laughed as he ran alongside Peter. They were headed toward Cook Street.

"Any word on who that might be?"

"I believe his name starts with a D."

"Huh. Very mysterious."

They continued along Dallas Road. Peter took quick snatches of moments to look out at the ocean. It looked majestic and powerful in winter. If you found yourself in it, it could kill you—quick. He had a lot of respect for the crashing waves and the creatures that lived beneath its surface.

"It's gorgeous," Danny said. "The scenery."

"This was a good idea." Peter dug deeper to keep up with Danny. The cold wasn't allowing his muscles to warm as they should. His thighs were burning.

"You doing all right?" Danny asked.

"As long as we keep a slow and steady pace, I'll be fine."

They crossed the road and headed down Cook Street. They'd jog through the village, then take a left on Southgate and go past Beacon Hill Park. Down Superior Street. Left on Government, then back along Dallas to their starting point.

They were running past the park when Peter grabbed Danny's arm and stopped.

Fuck.

The pain hurtling through his body startled him. It felt like someone had jammed a railway spike through his chest. Panic rolled through him.

Danny held Peter's shoulders as Peter gripped his chest. "What's going on?"

"I can't breathe," Peter whispered. "My chest ,,,," He bent forward. "Fuck!"

Peter felt like he was going to pass out.

Danny whipped out his phone, shed his gloves, and called 9-1-1. He put it on speakerphone so he could keep his focus on Peter. Peter sunk to his knees, clutching his chest. The call finally picked up. Danny kneeled beside Peter and put his hand on Peter's back. He put the phone on the ground. Peter couldn't pull in a proper breath. The pain was winding him.

"What service are you requesting?"

"Ambulance."

"One moment, please. I'll connect you."

Click. Click.

"What's your emergency?" The voice was just loud enough to hear.

"I think my partner is having a heart attack," Danny said.

"Are they conscious and breathing?"

"Yes."

"Are they on heart medication?"

"I have no idea."

Peter tapped Danny's leg and shook his head *no*.

"No, he isn't," Danny replied.

"How's his color?"

Danny leaned forward and looked at Peter's face. "It's dark. I can't see."

"Do you have aspirin?"

"No, we're out running."

"What's your location?"

"We're on Southgate near Douglas. The side near the park. We're on the sidewalk."

"Okay, I'm sending an ambulance to you. I'll stay on the phone with you until it arrives."

Peter groaned. It was the worst pain he'd ever felt. It spread to his shoulder. His left arm went numb. A lightning bolt of pain shot down it. He sucked in a small breath.

"Babe." Danny rubbed Peter's back. "What can I do?"

"That," Peter gasped. "Touch me."

Danny put his head against Peter's right shoulder. "Jeezus … don't you dare die on me."

"Love you," Peter managed to whisper. Danny needed to hear it in case it was the last time he was able to tell him. This felt bad. Really bad. Peter was surprised he was still conscious.

"I love you too. More and more each day. And we're going to have many, many more."

Peter could hear the sirens in the distance. It seemed forever until the ambulance pulled up on the curb alongside them. A second hand landed on his shoulder. Danny moved away from him.

"I'm Tim. And this is Cheryle. What's happening?" Peter was barely able to register he was being asked a question. He was slow to answer. He still felt as though he couldn't breathe.

"Pain. Chest. Arm. Can't breathe."

"Can you chew these for me?" The attendant Tim held two blue tablets in Peter's field of vision. Peter grabbed them and stuffed them into his mouth. They tasted horrible and dusty as he chewed them. Aspirin. He knew that. He did his best to grind them up before swallowing them.

"I need to test your oxygen level. Can I have a finger?"

Peter held out his hand. Tim removed his glove and placed a plastic clip on one of his fingers.

"Can I see your face?" Tim asked.

Peter lifted his head as best as he could. Tim flicked a flashlight across his face.

"Do you feel dizzy or nauseous?"

Peter nodded his head. This was taking way too long. He knew he needed to get to a hospital. The clip was removed from his finger. "We're going to start you on some oxygen then we're going to help you with that pain, okay? First, we're going to get you into the ambulance."

Finally.

"Can you stand?"

It took some effort and some help from both ambulance attendants, but Peter managed to struggle to his feet. He was directed toward a stretcher. It was lowered so it was easier for him to lie down. They raised it back up, covered him with a blanket, and strapped him to it.

The jarring motion as they loaded him into the ambulance made him feel sick. He hadn't moved his hand from his chest. Having it there didn't help. It was more of a comfort thing.

A plastic mask was placed on his face and elastic bands fixed over his ears.

"Can I come with him?"

Danny's voice.

"Are you family?"

"I'm his partner."

"Climb in."

Danny's cold bare hand slid into Peter's and clutched tight. "You're going to be all right."

The best Peter could do was groan.

"Let's deal with that pain," Tim said. The ambulance started up. The sirens sprung to life, and they started moving. "I need to start an IV, okay?"

Peter nodded. Tears streaked down his cheeks. He had never been so terrified. This could be it. His life could be over. He released his chest and set his arm by his side. Tim fussed around beside him. He barely felt the IV being placed in his arm.

"I'm going to get some morphine on board for you."

Peter looked over as the IV solution bag was hung from a hook and the tubing was attached to the cannula. Tim produced a needle and injected a port on the tubing.

"You should feel that in a few minutes," Tim said.

The rush of warmth was almost immediate. With each passing second, the pain in Peter's chest and arm waned. His breathing evened out. He took a deep breath. His chest felt tight.

The pain had shifted from sharp and horrific to a dull ache. It still hurt but it was manageable. He squeezed Danny's hand. "Feeling better," he mumbled from behind the mask.

"Thank God." Danny lifted their joined hands and kissed Peter's knuckles. "No more running for you. You nearly scared me to death."

"Too old," Peter whispered. He was. He was too old to be with someone like Danny. This proved it. He couldn't even participate in something Danny loved.

"Stop," Danny said. "Don't go there. You're stuck with me whether you like it or not. This is not going to change my mind." He kissed Peter's knuckles again. "I love you."

Peter sighed. If this didn't scare Danny off, nothing likely would. But a potential future of dementia and incontinence swirled through his mind. Would Danny stick around for that?

"Keep talking to him," Tim said.

Danny shifted closer and kissed Peter on the forehead. "I'm *never* going to leave you."

The ambulance pulled into the ambulance bay at the Royal Jubilee Hospital. The doors swung open, and Danny leaped out. Peter reached for Danny once the stretcher was loaded out. Danny came right to his side and clung to his hand. As they rolled Peter further into the hospital, Danny was told he would need to wait in the waiting room. Their hands slipped apart.

The next two hours were a blur. His mind was on Danny. He felt helplessly alone without him. People kept asking him questions. Electrodes were stuck all over his chest. Nurses and doctors whisked in and out of the curtained area they had placed him in. Blood draws. More medication.

It was confirmed he'd had a heart attack.

He was admitted and just needed to wait for a bed.

The curtain pulled back, and Danny walked through the opening. Peter lifted the oxygen mask away from his face. "You didn't run on me." He made his best effort at a smile.

Danny grinned. "I told you. Not going anywhere." He pulled up a chair, sat by Peter's bedside, and reached for Peter's hand. Danny's hand felt warm this time.

"I *did* have a heart attack."

"Yeah, the doctor told me."

"Good. I'm glad they talked to you. I told them you were my emergency contact."

Danny kissed Peter's wrist. "I'll always be here for you." Danny's phone buzzed. He lifted it from his pocket. "I texted Samuel. This will be him."

Danny leaned back in his chair.

"Hey, Samuel."

Pause.

"Yeah, he's all right. Heart attack."

Pause.

"I'm with him right now."

Pause.

"We were out for a run together."

Pause.

Danny scowled.

"The doctor said the running brought it on but didn't cause it."

Pause.

"He's not too old."

Pause.

"He has high blood pressure and high cholesterol. It was always a possibility."

Pause.

"Yes, the doctor talked to me."

Pause.

"Because I'm here with him."

Pause.

"Because … I told you … we were out running."

Pause.

"He's under a lot of stress. I thought a run would be good for him."

Pause.

Danny furrowed his brows. Anger sparked in his eyes.

"Fuck off, Samuel. I didn't cause this."

Pause.

"You'll have to wait to visit until he has a room."

Pause.

"Because he is only allowed one visitor back here and I'm not leaving."

Pause.

Danny sighed.

"Fine. We can switch off."

No.

Peter shook his head. He didn't want Danny to go. He wanted to see his son but Samuel could wait until he was in a room to see him. He squeezed Danny's hand and shook his head again.

"Hold, on, Samuel."

Danny held the microphone against his chest. "You don't want me to leave?"

"Please don't."

Danny lifted the phone back to his ear. "Your dad doesn't want me to leave."

Pause.

"None of your business. That's what your dad wants. I'll call you when he has a room."

Pause.

"I'm hanging up now, Samuel. You can swear at me when your dad is feeling better."

Danny closed the call.

"He's not happy," Danny said. "Wants to know why you want me here."

Peter lifted the oxygen mask from his face. "We can't tell him."

Danny sighed. "I know."

A nurse poked her head in. "We have a bed for you in ICU." She stepped back to let the hospital porter in. The curtain was pulled away and locks released on the bed.

"I'll follow," Danny said.

Peter was rolled down hallway after hallway. An elevator ride and more hallways. His bed was finally turned into a room with a glass wall facing a nurses' station.

"You'll need to transfer onto this bed." The porter patted a bed in the center of the room. He pulled the stretcher bed up beside it. "I'll help you."

It took a few tries, but Peter finally climbed onto the bed and got the gown organized they had changed him into in the emergency room. He was switched over to an oxygen canula.

Then he was left alone with Danny.

"Thank you for staying with me," Peter mumbled.

"I wouldn't be anywhere else."

Peter closed his eyes. He was exhausted. The doctor was confident he wouldn't have another heart attack any time soon. That gave him some comfort. They'd started him on blood thinners.

Danny's voice barely registered. From what he could discern, Danny was on the phone telling Samuel what room number he was in. Something about a ten-minute limit.

Peter's mind buzzed. He was slipping off into sleep.

"No, that doesn't apply to me."

Danny's voice, still on the phone.

Pause.

"Goddam it, Samuel. Mind your own fucking business."

It sounded like their secret was unraveling. It was only a matter of time until Samuel found out about Danny and him. Lying there, he had a change of heart. He no longer cared.

Danny was the man he loved.

He trusted whatever decision Danny made.

Pause.

Pause.

Maybe the phone call was over.

Peter awoke to the sound of Samuel's voice. There was no longer light shining through the window. The room was dimly lit. He turned his head. Danny was sitting in a chair against the wall.

"Hey, Dad." Samuel touched his shoulder. "How are you feeling?"

"Groggy," Peter grunted.

"You scared us."

"Scared myself."

"What the hell were you doing out running?"

"Clearing my head."

"Next time just have a drink or something."

Peter frowned. Samuel was treating him like an aging invalid. He jogged every other day on his treadmill. Danny was right. It could have easily happened at home. While he was alone. He was blessed to have been with Danny.

He turned his head and smiled at Danny.

Danny shot him a wink back.

Samuel only caught the first half of the interaction. He looked over his shoulder at Danny.

"What are you still doing here?" Samuel asked Danny.

"I told you. I'm not leaving."

Samuel frowned. "Why the hell do you care so much about my dad."

Danny rose to his feet. "We got to know each other at the real estate conference."

Samuel looked back and forth between Peter and Danny. His eyes widened. "You?" he pointed at Danny. His face flushed crimson. "You're the guy my dad hooked up with?"

Danny simply shrugged.

Samuel launched himself at Danny and pinned him to the wall. "You sick fuck!"

Peter struggled to sit. He wanted to go to Danny's defense. He threw the blankets off and freed his feet. He gripped the bedrail and swung one leg off the bed.

Danny knocked Samuel's arms out of the way and ran to the edge of the bed.

"Don't." Danny supported Peter's legs and swung him back into bed. "You're not supposed to get up." Samuel grabbed Danny's shoulder. Danny rolled it away from Samuel's grasp.

Danny turned on Samuel after he had Peter settled.

"This is not the time for this," he said and reached for Peter's hand. He clutched it. The look on Samuel's face was a mix of anger and confusion. His face was still red, eyebrows crumpled above glaring eyes. He ran his hand through his hair and clutched a clump.

"No way," Samuel said. "You are going to tell me what's going on." He released his hair and pointed at their joined hands. "That … that there. What the fuck?"

"It wasn't a one-night stand," Peter said.

"I don't understand," Samuel said and shook his head. "You've been seeing him, Dad?"

"We spent most of our time together at the conference," Danny said.

Samuel shoved Danny. "I didn't ask you … traitor."

"We kept seeing each other after Vegas," Peter said. "We made an undeniable connection. We couldn't let it go … our desire to be together. We tried. Knew it would cause problems."

Peter squeezed Danny's hand. It was the right decision to continue their journey together. "The thought of losing him was too painful."

Samuel's jaw jutted out as he eyed up Danny. "He's old enough to be your father."

"Age hasn't been an issue," Danny replied.

"Until now," Samuel countered.

"It's not going to stop us." Danny rested his hip against the bed. "I'm in love with your dad."

Samuel coughed out a laugh. "Love?"

"I love him right back," Peter said. "It was quick, but I've never been surer about anything in my life." It was true. His love for Danny was seated in his soul.

Samuel scrubbed his hand across his mouth. "Bullshit! You're delusional." He stabbed a finger at Danny. "He's manipulated you into being a goddamned cradle robber."

Danny's face flushed with a ruddy red color. "Why the hell would I do that?"

"I don't know. Daddy issues."

"My dad and I have a strong relationship."

"So then, why do you need mine?"

Danny turned and stroked the side of Peter's face. "I love him, Samuel. There's nothing more to it than that. He completes me. He compliments me. He opposes me in the best ways possible."

"I'm not accepting this." Samuel threw up his hands.

"That's your choice," Peter said. "Ours has been made."

"Then you're on your own. The both of you." Samuel turned and left the room. Tears slipped down Peter's face. It was his worst fear that Samuel would disown him.

Danny brushed away Peter's tears with his thumb.

"He'll come around," Danny said.

Peter patted the edge of the bed and shifted his body over against the left guardrail.

"Come up here," he said.

Danny released Peter's hand and climbed onto the bed. Peter lay his right arm out and Danny nestled on top of it, his face tucked against his favorite spot on Peter's neck. Danny placed his hand on Peter's stomach. It was the contact Peter needed.

He turned his face and kissed Danny's hair.

"You are my everything," Peter said.

"And you're mine." Danny lifted his head. "I'm not hurting you?"

"My chest is a bit sore but you're good where you are."

Danny snuggled in. Lifted one leg to drape over Peter's thigh. It was late. It would be morning soon. Peter hummed against Danny's forehead.

Danny's breathing slowed and he stopped stroking Peter's stomach. Peter smiled at the ceiling. Danny was asleep. Peter could imagine every night for the rest of his life being like this.

Chapter Nine | Danny

When Danny woke, Peter was asleep. His breathing was strong and steady. The room was bright. He vaguely remembered a nurse coming in to check on Peter and take his blood pressure a few times throughout the night. He was thankful they hadn't asked him to get off the bed.

He closed his eyes and relaxed. He could sleep longer.

"Oh, you have got to be fucking kidding me. Samuel wasn't lying."

Danny rolled to look over his shoulder.

Peter's best friend, Maxwell, and his son, Ryan, were standing at the bedside behind him. It was Ryan who had spoken. Maxwell approached the bed; a look of concern painted his face like a Greek theatre tragedy mask. He placed his hand on Peter's foot.

"How's he doing?" Maxwell asked Danny.

"Better. They've given him meds to stop another heart attack."

"Samuel said he was out running out with you."

"Yeah, we were burning off a bit of stress."

"Do you think the stress caused this?" Maxwell asked.

"He had some health conditions that contributed."

"His high blood pressure?"

"Amongst other things."

It wasn't his place to give Maxwell Peter's entire medical history. He'd been in the room for every consultation with the emergency doctor. He knew a lot more about Peter's health now.

Peter was going to be around for a long time now that his heart was being treated.

"Hey." Peter opened his eyes. He scanned the room and smiled at Maxwell. "You didn't have to come. I'm doing all right. Danny and the nurses have been keeping an eye on me."

"Of course, I had to come." Maxwell patted Peter's ankle.

Danny removed himself from the mattress to give Maxwell room to approach the head of the bed. He pulled up a chair for Maxwell to sit on. Maxwell sat and gripped Peter's hand.

Danny nudged Ryan. "Let's leave them alone."

"Yeah. I have questions. Let's grab a coffee."

They walked in silence to the coffee shop located at the main entrance and placed their orders. They waited, grabbed their coffees, and found a table to sit at.

"Fire away," Danny said.

"You and Peter … you're together? Like together—together?"

"We spent a lot of time with each other at the real estate conference. We clicked."

"He's old enough to be your father. What on earth do you see in him?"

Danny smiled. "He's kind. He's caring. He's smart … and funny. We share a lot of the same ambitions and fears. We have so much in common. Likes and dislikes. Passions. Plus, he sees me. He hears me. He remembers little things about me. I matter to him. *We* matter to him."

Ryan leaned back in his chair. "Samuel mentioned you said you were in love."

"We are."

"How did that happen?"

"So easily. We talked for hours and hours. Time flew by

with him. We couldn't get enough of each other's company. That combined with the physical stuff … we fell in love."

Ryan sighed. "It's fucking weird, man. My dad is floored."

"He didn't show it."

"He's stoic that way. I'm sure he and Peter are having a heart-to-heart." Ryan took a sip of coffee and then returned the cup to the table. "I didn't know Peter was into men."

"It's not my place to say what his sexuality is."

"My dad always suspected Peter was gay."

Danny furrowed his brow. "Why?"

"Ever since high school, Peter let his eyes wander toward guys. It was obvious to my dad that Peter was attracted to them. He's not surprised Peter finally fulfilled his orientation." Ryan leaned forward. "But you … Dad was not expecting that. You're almost the same age as Samuel."

"We've discussed that at length."

"And you decided to go through with it … alienate Peter's son."

"We're in love. Samuel will need to find a way to accept that."

"What if he doesn't?"

"Then Peter will be devastated. But it won't change how he feels about me."

"You're sure of that?"

"We're bonded. We're partners in every way. Neither of us is going anywhere."

"You sound awfully sure of that."

"I feel it in my soul … so does he."

Ryan offered a small smile. "I needed to make sure you weren't taking advantage of Peter. He's still grieving for his wife. He's vulnerable."

"He still has his moments. They were together for a long

time. I do my best to give him space when the memories of her sweep in. Usually, he prefers to talk it through with me."

"Does that feel weird … talking about his wife?"

"His time with her helped shape him into the amazing man he is today."

"You really are in love with him, aren't you?"

"To my very core."

"Then Samuel is an idiot for walking away if you make each other that happy. I'll talk to him. See if I can make some inroads into his acceptance of your relationship."

"Appreciate it." Danny finished his coffee. "I need to get back to Peter. They're going to let him go home tomorrow. Gonna hold off on a shower until then."

"Can I get you a change of clothes at least? You could get out of that running gear."

"That would be amazing." Danny dug around in a pocket of his sweatshirt and produced a set of keys. "Something comfortable. Sweats and a t-shirt, and a sweater."

Ryan grabbed the keys. "Done. I'll bring them around in thirty or so. I suspect my dad will want to stay until then." He stood as Danny rose to his feet. Ryan made his way around to Danny's side of the table and wrapped him up in his arms. "I don't care about the stigma you are walking into. I'm happy for you." He laughed in Danny's ear. "Last person I thought would settle down."

Danny smiled and tugged Ryan to him. "Thank you … for everything."

Ryan stepped away. "Got your back, man." He retreated to the sliding doors and left the hospital. Danny stuffed his hands into his sweatshirt pockets and headed for the elevators. At least Ryan supported them. Samuel might come around. It had to have been shocking to find out that way. To walk into a room and discover your dad's lover and partner hovering by his bedside.

Samuel had called him a traitor. It was true. In some way, he had betrayed their friendship, but not deliberately. He wouldn't have set about pursuing Peter. They had fallen into it naturally.

It felt destined.

Danny walked back into Peter's room. Maxwell was at Peter's bedside holding his hand. Peter had his eyes closed but he was still talking in a whisper.

"Danny means everything to me," Peter said to Maxwell.

Danny approached the other side of the bed, bent forward and kissed Peter's forehead, then took his other hand. He stroked his thumb back and forth across it.

Peter's eyes fluttered open. "Did you have a good talk with Ryan?"

"Yeah." Danny smiled. "He's all good. He's picking me up some clothes."

"Hon … you should go home. Have a shower and something to eat."

Danny shook his head. "I'm not leaving you."

"You're so stubborn."

"When it comes to you … yes."

Maxwell stood. "I'm going to go." He looked at Danny. "Take care of him."

"I will," Danny replied.

After Maxwell left the room, Danny snatched the opportunity to kiss Peter. The heat was there under the haze of exhaustion. It would be weeks until they could consummate their love again, but Danny didn't mind waiting. He had all the time in the world for Peter.

He pulled up a chair and took a seat.

"I want you to come back to my place when you're discharged … so I can keep an eye on you. The doctor said it's either that or you have community care workers coming in at all times of the day to check on you. I'd rather you were at my place. Or I could stay at yours."

"I'd rather be at home."

"Yours it is then."

"Are you sure you want to do that? Don't you have things to do?"

"I can set up in your office. Have other agents do my showings. I'll be fine."

Peter reached out and stroked Danny's face. "You're too good to me."

"Nonsense. You're my partner. I'm here for you."

Peter closed his eyes but kept Danny's face cupped in his hand. "I need to sleep. Maxwell wore me out with a game of twenty questions."

"He cares about you."

"Deeply."

"I'm glad you have him. Sounds like he's always come through for you." Danny leaned into the touch of Peter's hand. "What did he think … about us?"

"He was confused. He knew I liked men. Couldn't understand why I'd picked you to experiment with at the conference. I filled him in on how it was never just sexual."

Danny turned and kissed Peter's palm. "Get some sleep. I'll be right over there." He pointed at the sofa-turned bed in the corner of the room. "I need to catch some sleep myself."

Peter was already nearly asleep. Danny slipped away to the bed and tucked himself under a layer of blankets one of the nurses had brought in for him. Sleep didn't come easy, but his body finally submitted. When he woke, a set of clothes and his keys were at the foot of the bed.

Danny had been living at Peter's for three weeks. It was long past when he needed to be there, but he couldn't tear himself away. They'd grown even closer during their time living together. He never could have imagined they could become woven like a piece of fine linen. So tight they appeared as a solid sheet of exquisite material. He snuggled against Peter on the sofa.

"I need to head into the office again tomorrow," Danny said. He hated to do it, to leave Peter, but he had a business to run, and he could only expect his team to fill in for him for so long. His dreams of starting his own agency had been put on hold while Peter recuperated.

"No problem. I'll be fine." Peter closed the laptop he had been tapping away on for hours. He'd started working two weeks ago. Slow and small at first. Now he was up to his usual workload.

There was no reason for Danny to remain living with him.

Except one.

He couldn't bear to be without Peter. Falling asleep with him each night. Waking up at his side each morning. Spending their day together. Touching—kissing ... loving each other.

"I'll be home by 7 to cook dinner," Danny said.

"You don't have to keep doing that. I can cook."

"I know you can cook ... but I want to do it."

Peter reached for Danny's hand. "I'm good now, you know."

Danny frowned. "You don't want me here anymore?" An ache of rejection washed into his chest. They were supposed to be in love—partners. Was Peter pushing him away?

"We should get back to normal. I feel great," Peter said.

Panic rose in Danny's throat. By the sounds of it, Peter wanted him gone—today. He wasn't ready to leave. He would never be ready to leave him. A million thoughts whirred through his mind. Maybe Peter wasn't in love with him anymore. Maybe he'd been delusional to think they'd grown closer. Had he been blind to Peter's decision to withdraw?

"But …." Tears stung Danny's eyes. Peter studied him and frowned.

"What is it?"

Danny clung to Peter's hand. "I don't want to go. I want to stay here with you." He stared down at their hands. It needed to be asked. He looked up. "Do you not love me anymore?"

Peter's eyes grew wide. "Of course, I do." He struggled from Danny's embrace on his hand and lifted his hands to cup Danny's face. "I thought you'd be sick of taking care of me."

Danny shook his head. "Never. I want to stay with you forever."

Peter's eyebrows dipped. "Do you want to move in?"

That was something Danny had been playing with in his mind. Moving in together. It seemed like the natural progression of their relationship. When two people loved each other, they wanted to spend as much time as possible with each other, right? You could only truly do that by living together. Danny looked around. He didn't think he could live in Peter's house, though.

"I want to move in together," Danny replied. "But could it be my place?"

Peter sighed, then surveyed the room. "I'd like that. There are too many memories of my wife here. Good times with Samuel growing up too. But mostly sadness."

Danny's heart swelled with excitement. This was a huge step. A step toward what … he wasn't sure. What he was sure of was they would do it as a couple. He nearly bounced off the sofa. "Then I need to head home and start clearing some room in my closet."

"It'll take me a while to get fully organized. There are details to work out. Do I sell the house? Do I rent it out? Furnished? Not furnished? What I want to bring with me. What will fit."

Danny sat back on the sofa. "Lots to think about."

"I can move in with you while I'm working through those things, though."

"You're sure?"

"I don't want to be anywhere else." Peter smiled. "Besides, your house is nicer than mine."

"I thought you didn't like all the glass and steel." Danny rose to his feet. "Maybe we can buy something different together. Someplace to call home that we both like."

Peter grinned. "I'd love to do that with you." He brushed his hands back and forth together. "One decision made. I'll sell this house so we can afford something nice."

Danny tucked his lips between his teeth as he restrained a smile that would've ripped his face in two. "We're really doing this."

"We are."

"Uplands?"

Peter laughed. "If we can find something in our price range."

"Oh, I'll find something."

"I have no doubt in my mind about that."

"I'll sell my place when we find something new. It'll go quicker than your place. I'll get to work on it right away finding us a dream home. You can organize selling this property."

Danny bent down for a kiss. It was hard to pull away.

They'd just agreed to a whole new level of commitment. He peeled himself away and brushed his thumb down the center of Peter's bottom lip. "God, you taste good. I can't wait to taste more of you."

"Soon." Peter grinned. "I have that appointment with the cardiologist tomorrow. Hopefully, he will give me the go-ahead. Now, go and get that massive house of yours ready for me."

Danny crossed his fingers for luck and held them above his head as he backed out of the room. "See you later, babe." He jogged down the stairs, out the door, and to his car.

He shrieked aloud in his car; his heart filled with joy. They were starting a life together. A real life. Not just moving in together. They would be sharing title on a massive asset.

For the first time in his life, he felt secure. He'd spent his entire adult life chasing money. Trying to achieve that feeling of stability. Now, he'd found it. Not in money and success but in the arms of an incredible man. They just needed to get from here to there.

There was so much work to be done.

Danny pulled into his driveway. His house didn't feel as cold as it usually did when he stepped through the front door. It would soon be a home. A home he shared with the man of his dreams. Then they'd find something that mixed their two styles. Cozy and chic combined.

He started with his closet. It was already massive. He'd modified a small bedroom next to the master bedroom. It only took a bit of placing clothing items a little closer together to clear some room for Peter's extensive wardrobe. The same went for the drawers in the dressing closet. A little reorganizing freed up an entire side of the island drawer cabinet. They'd manage.

The bathroom was next. Then the office. That was going to be trickier. He was going to have to turn the second den into an office for one of them. He wandered into the kitchen. Peter had a lot of kitchenware that he was very particular about. They'd need to pack up everything Peter wanted to keep, then fit it amongst Danny's already well-equipped kitchen.

Danny poured himself a drink and reclined on his lounge chair. He looked at the dark cold fireplace. Soon he and Peter would be sitting in front of its warm flames.

He lifted his phone.

<Danny: "I'm all ready for you.">

<Peter: "That was fast.">

<Danny: "I'm motivated.">

<Peter: "I'll come by after my doctor's appointment tomorrow.">

<Danny: "To stay over?">

<Peter: "That's what I'm hoping.">

<Danny: "When should we move you in?">

<Peter: "Wednesday? Depends on when I can get a truck for all the wardrobe boxes.">

<Danny: "How many are we talking about?">

<Peter: "Don't give me any guff. You're as bad as me.">

<Danny:> *<Smile emoji>*

<Peter: "Wednesday should work. I have a favor to call in.">

<Danny: "Perfect. I'll make sure we have ingredients for a nice dinner.">

<Peter: "Love you. See you tomorrow.">

*<Danny: "I'll be ready and waiting for you.">**<Wink emoji>*

Chapter Ten | Danny

Danny checked his phone. Peter's appointment with the cardiologist had been at 3 pm. It was now 3:30. He knew he was being impatient, but he wanted to know his love was all right.

He paced the living room. There was nothing more important right now than Peter's health. They had plans. Not just their love life. They had talked about Peter joining Danny's real estate agency venture when it finally took off. He would be an incredible asset. Peter had a lucrative client list. They were twining their lives together. Danny wanted their time together to be long.

His phone buzzed.

<Peter: "Be there in 15.">

<Danny: "What did the doctor say?">

<Peter: "Good to go.">

<Danny: "Like ...."><Eggplant emoji>

<Peter:><Laughing crying emoji><"Yes.">

<Danny: "Drive faster.">

Pause.

<Danny: "No, wait ... don't. Safety first.">

<Peter: "Getting into my car. See you soon.">

Danny wasn't sure what to do first. He hadn't wanted to get his hopes up that he could turn his love for Peter into something physical today. His stomach fluttered. They hadn't been together in almost a month. He headed upstairs to stage the bedroom. Peter deserved candlelight.

He whipped the room-darkening curtains closed in the bedroom and pitched it into darkness. The closet with the candles was down the hall. He worked quickly to light as many as he could. He ended up with twenty-seven. The exact number of years difference in their age. He contemplated adding another or blowing one out. He decided to leave them.

It had significance. It represented each year between them that was lit with ethereal light. A bridge of steady shimmering warmth. Burning strong.

The chime announcing the opening of Danny's front door sounded. He raced to the balcony overlooking the front entry. "I'm upstairs."

"I see you're not wasting any time." Peter smiled as he kicked off his shoes and ascended the stairs. "What makes you think I'm even in the mood?"

Danny draped his arms around Peter's neck. "Babe, don't tease me."

"I thought you'd be undressed already."

"I was going to get you to do that."

"Were you going to *tell* me to?" Peter asked.

Danny hummed as he watched Peter. "Do you want me to … *tell* you?"

Peter groaned and wrapped his arms around Danny's waist. He tugged Danny to him. "You know I'll do anything you want. All you have to do is tell me what you need from me."

Danny jammed his hand into the hair at the back of Peter's head. He clung to him, tipped his head, and kissed him—hard. He pulled back. Peter's pupils were blown wide.

"Anytime you want me to stop, I'll stop," Danny said. "Traffic light rules."

"What's that?"

"Red means stop. Yellow means take a break … green

means go."

Peter tucked his face against the nape of Danny's neck. "Then green. Please green."

"You'll need to listen to me. You'll need to behave."

"I can do that."

"Let's go to the bedroom." Danny took Peter's hand and led him through the door. He turned Peter until the back of Peter's legs were against the bed.

Danny unbuttoned Peter's jeans, then slid them down his legs until they were wrapped around his thighs. Peter stepped back and forth until the jeans fell to his ankles.

"Don't do that," Danny said and lifted the jeans back up. "Spread your legs so they stay there." He patted the bed. "Sit down." Peter did what he was told and sat on the edge of the bed.

Danny pushed on Peter's chest until Peter got the message and lay down; his feet still on the floor; the position of his jeans restricting his ability to spread his legs. Danny kneeled on the floor between Peter's legs and mouthed his balls through the fabric of Peter's underpants.

Peter groaned and ran his fingers through Danny's hair.

"Don't." Danny gripped Peter's wrists. "Don't touch anything. Put your hands behind your head." Danny released Peter's wrists and Peter lifted his hands and wove his fingers together behind his head as he'd been told to do. Peter's immediate submission hardened Danny's cock. Peter was playing right along. Peter needed this release in his life. Danny was going to take care of him.

Danny kissed the underside of Peter's hard cock. "What color are you at?"

"Green. Absolutely green."

"Good." Danny went back to teasing Peter's balls through

the thin material. Then nuzzled his nose along Peter's shaft. "You smell amazing." He used his lips to caress Peter's cockhead. The firm cap was trapped just beneath the waistband of Peter's underwear.

Danny slipped his fingers beneath the band and released the straining cock into the air. Peter hissed and squirmed as Danny licked the slit, ever so slowly. He sucked at it, then lowered his mouth and pressed Peter's head all the way down his throat. He didn't have a gag reflex anymore. He loved sucking cock and took advantage of any opportunity he was presented with.

He closed his lips around Peter's length and used his tongue to increase the pressure as he slurped Peter to the tip. He gripped the root and dove back on. He looked up along the length of Peter's body. The trail of hair up his stomach, the silver hair on his chest, the piercing steely grey-blue eyes watching him. Peter's mouth hung open with ecstasy.

That's the way Danny wanted to keep Peter forever. Suspended in bliss. He kept working as Peter clenched and unclenched his ass, raising his erection up and down into Danny's mouth.

Danny decided to allow it.

"Danny …." Peter whispered. "I'm gonna …."

Danny slid his lips until only the tip of Peter's cock was in his mouth. Then he let that slip out. Peter's cock bobbed above his stomach. Danny kissed the base of the tight shaft.

"Then we better take a break," Danny said.

The groan emitted by Peter made Danny smile. He had no intention of letting Peter cum anytime soon. He was serious about suspending Peter's bliss. His bliss and his release.

Danny took his time removing Peter's jeans, his underwear, then his socks.

"Shuffle up the bed."

Danny followed Peter there and lay down beside him. He encouraged Peter to roll closer and into his arms. Peter snuggled in. His head on Danny's chest; his hand on Danny's stomach.

"Tell me everything the doctor told you," Danny said.

"Um ... okay." Danny felt Peter swallow hard. Edging him was going to be fun. Peter stroked the fabric of Danny's shirt. "Those tests I had last week look promising. The medication is doing its job but just in case, he gave me a sample of a *rescue med*. If I have chest pains, I'm supposed to administer it, then call 9-1-1. But he's fairly confident I won't need it."

"That makes me so happy ... and relieved. I want you around for as long as possible." Danny turned his head and kissed Peter's hair. "Undo my shirt for me."

Peter was quick to comply. His fingers made fast work of Danny's buttons. He spread Danny's shirt open and stroked his chest. His hand stopped on Danny's nipple. He caressed it between two fingers, then leaned over to take it into his mouth.

Danny touched Peter's shoulder and stopped him. "Remember what I told you about touching." Danny removed himself from the bed. "Lay flat on your back."

Peter did as he was told. "Pull your knees up. Hook your arms behind your knees to keep them there. I want you to display your hole while I get undressed." Danny's cock throbbed as he watched Peter arrange himself. His ass looked like it was meant to be there.

Ready and waiting.

Danny shed his clothes. Peter watched him. He crawled onto the end of the bed and toward Peter. This would be similar to Peter's first sexual experience with him as a gay man, but Danny was going to expand on that. He was going to take Peter to the very edge and no further.

He used his thumbs to pull open the tight ring of muscle then dipped his tongue in as far as it would go. It tightened away from his tongue. "I need you to relax."

Peter unclenched. Danny took a swipe with his tongue. Peter tasted musky and all male. It was intoxicating—the feel and the taste. He licked and prodded until Peter's legs started shaking.

Danny licked one of his fingers and fingered Peter's hole. It clamped down on his finger, but he kept up the thrust and retreat until Peter opened for him. He removed his finger and licked Peter's hole, then wet two fingers. This time Peter was ready for him.

Peter groaned and whispered, "Fuck, yeah."

"What color?"

"Purple."

Danny smiled. "And what does purple mean?"

"It means I'm blissed out and don't want you to ever stop."

"That's a good color." Danny spat at Peter's hole, then massaged it into Peter's hole with three fingers. Peter's body objected for a split second, then sucked him in.

"You're being very good," Danny said and abandoned Peter's ass. He stretched over until his hand was on the drawer of his bedside table. He removed a bottle of lube from its depths.

"Let me hold your leg up," Danny said. "Hold out your hand." He took over keeping Peter's leg raised in the air and squeezed a dollop of lube into Peter's outstretched hand.

"You can stroke yourself. But you need to tell me if you're going to cum."

Peter set to work, sliding his soft fist up and down his shaft. His hips undulated, pumping his cock up and down into his hand. Peter's eyes were closed.

"Open your eyes," Danny said. "Don't take your eyes off mine."

Peter's eyes fluttered open. They were dominated by his pupils. His stare was intense; not blinking often. Danny licked his lips. He could taste Peter on them.

"Pump faster," Danny said. "Fuck your hand hard."

Peter increased his speed. His breathing changed and he was having trouble maintaining eye contact. He was close. "Stop," Danny said.

Peter's eyes widened, pleading. His hand slowed. He set it on the bed beside him.

"Good boy."

Peter bit his bottom lip and groaned. This was doing something for him. Danny still didn't know everything about Peter, but obeying was fulfilling something Peter needed.

"You can put your legs down."

Peter lowered his legs.

Danny straddled Peter's hips, then he crawled up the bed until his knees were on Peter's pillow and he was staring down at him. He tapped his hard cock on Peter's lips.

"Are you going to be good and take this whole thing?"

Peter nodded. That was likely all he could do; he was so worked up. Peter's mouth popped open, and he extended his tongue. It was a sight, Peter looking up at him—submitting to him.

Danny grabbed the top of the headboard and fed Peter his cock. He didn't stop until his balls were pressed against Peter's chin. To his credit, Peter didn't cough. Danny withdrew then thrust in deep. This time Peter gagged for a second. The guttural sound wound Danny up.

He gripped the headboard and pumped his cock in and out of Peter's mouth. Peter moved his hands and placed them on

Danny's ass.

Danny stopped thrusting.

"What did I say about touching? Reach up and grab the headboard." It was a feature of Danny's bed. He had deliberately bought a bed with spindles on the headboard. It offered the opportunity to restrain his lovers, whether by ropes, handcuffs, or self-restraint like he was asking of Peter.

Peter raised his arms and gripped the headboard.

Danny fell into a steady rhythm.

He tipped his head and stared at the ceiling, then back down to watch his cock sliding in and out of Peter's mouth. He grunted. Peter's mouth was taking him too close to release.

"Watch your arms," Danny said. "I'm climbing off. Don't want to hurt you."

Peter tucked his arms in and let Danny shimmy off him.

Danny was back at the bedside table. He retrieved a condom. He held it up so Peter could see it. "I'm going to use this … on you. What color does that bring up for you?"

He sat astride Peter's hips.

Peter's chest rose and fell more dramatically than it had been doing a second before.

"I … I don't know."

Danny tipped his head to one side. "You know how much I love you."

"It's a big step. I never thought of myself as a bottom."

"You responded so well to my prepping you."

Peter furrowed his brow. "I didn't realize that was what you were doing."

"Did you like me filling you with my fingers?"

Peter groaned out a "God, yeah," and reached for Danny's face but then thought better of it. He placed his hand down on his chest, then back down on the bed.

"You can give me the red light if you want," Danny said. "I'm not going to order you to do it. You have to want it." He stroked Peter's face. "But I want to share this with you."

Peter licked his lips. "You'll be gentle?"

"I would never do anything to hurt you."

Peter squirmed beneath Danny. Peter's hard cock pulsed against the crease of Danny's ass and between his balls. "Then … it's a brilliant green light."

Danny smiled, leaned down, and kissed Peter. The kiss was long and deep, filled with desire and the promise of a new connection. He sat back and ripped the condom package open. He removed the condom and held it out to Peter. "Put it on me."

The sensation nearly overwhelmed him; Peter rolling a condom onto him. His delicate fingers and firm grip nearly brought him to the very edge. Under Peter's watchful eye, Danny moved Peter's hands away and coated his sensitive cock with lube. He moved back and eased his knees between Peter's. Peter lifted his legs, held up by his hands, and created the perfect target.

Danny circled Peter's tight ring with his cockhead, then sank in a short way. Peter gasped and clenched up. "Calm, babe. It'll be worth it, I promise."

Peter relaxed and Danny slid in further—slow and easy. Every few seconds, he gave Peter a chance to adjust until his cock was seated deep inside Peter's ass.

"What color is your light?" Danny asked.

"Yellow."

"Okay." Danny prompted Peter to lower his legs and Danny adjusted his body until he was lying flat out on Peter's chest. "We'll just rest here until you're ready."

He kept his cock buried deep. As long as they weren't there

too long, he would stay hard.

"Can I touch you?" Peter said.

"You can hold me."

Peter folded Danny into his arms. Danny tucked his face into the space behind Peter's ear that was slowly becoming his safe space. He felt at peace there.

They just breathed for a few minutes.

"Green," Peter whispered.

Gently, Danny raised himself onto one elbow and pumped his hips back, then forward. Peter groaned and dug his nails into Danny's shoulders.

It was on the tip of Danny's tongue to tell Peter to reach for the headboard again. He decided to leave that for another time. The image of Peter tied and gagged floated through his mind.

Not today.

Today was special. Today was about love. About two men who loved each other playing with a bit of submission. Having love flow back and forth between them.

Danny angled his hips and picked up his pace. He sucked and licked Peter's neck. The sounds Peter was making—he could feel the vibration in his lips. He lifted one of Peter's legs and changed his angle. He wanted Peter to cum without touching himself.

"Oh … God … Danny." Peter ran his hand into Danny's hair and clutched Danny's head to him. Danny shifted his position again until Peter couldn't contain a long, sultry wail.

"Can I?" Peter whispered. "Please."

Danny nipped at Peter's ear. "Can you what?"

A moment of hesitation. "Can I cum?"

He knew those words had never been uttered by Peter before. Asking permission to do something his body was screaming to do.

"Only if I can taste it afterward," Danny replied.

Peter grunted and clung tighter to Danny's head. He pumped his hips in time to Danny's thrusts. Danny sucked in a breath as Peter's ass clamped down hard around his cock. He kept his pace. Peter tipped his head back, closed his eyes, grunted, and came.

Danny lowered Peter's leg and switched to bringing himself the full pleasure he desired. He pumped harder and faster until the release he'd been denying himself for a month nearly made him pass out, it was so intense. He definitely saw stars. He collapsed beside Peter.

Peter rolled against his side.

"Hold up," Danny said. "You made me a promise." He ran his finger through the cum on Peter's belly before it was lost in an embrace. He lifted his finger and smeared a taste along Peter's lips. Peter was quick to lick it away. Peter accepted Danny's finger as it was placed in his mouth. He closed his lips and sucked and tongued Danny's finger. Peter hummed with satisfaction.

"Good boy," Danny said.

Danny slipped his finger from Peter's mouth, ran it through the mess on Peter's skin, and then popped it into his own mouth. "Mmm … perfectly delicious."

"I love you," Peter whispered and cupped Danny's face. He took control of Danny's lips. Danny returned the loving connection. He couldn't imagine being anywhere else.

He gripped the back of Peter's neck and separated from his lips.

"I love you too."

This was a love that was going to last. He could feel it in the depths of his soul.

Chapter Eleven | Peter

"Let me get this straight." Samuel was furious. The blue ridges of veins were prominent on his face. "You're going to sell our family home, the home I grew up in, and set up house with a man thirty years younger than you that you've only known for what … five weeks!"

"Yes, that's the plan. Danny and I are going to find a home we both like."

"You're going to take your money … money you have worked many hard years for and combine it with someone you've barely spent any time with."

"We've spent enough time together to know we love each other."

Samuel shoved his hand into his hair. "Please don't say that around me." He walked in a quick circle, then came back to face Peter. "You're going to take out a mortgage with him."

"That's usually the way it works. We won't have enough money to buy outright."

"And remind me why that is again."

"Danny wants a house in Uplands."

"Danny wants … do you give Danny everything he wants."

Peter thought back to the night they'd had last weekend. Danny had taken complete control of him. He had done everything Danny asked of him.

Then they'd switched roles.

"We're partners. There's give and take on both sides."

"And what are you getting out of this … and opportunity to

tap some young ass?"

Peter scowled. "That's uncalled for. It's not about sex. What we have is deeper than that."

"See … I don't believe that for a second. Danny wants something."

"Don't be ridiculous."

Samuel poked his finger against Peter's chest. "Has he been asking you to marry him?"

A little panic ran through Peter's chest. But he contained it. It was unfounded. But he'd be lying if he said he hadn't considered it.

"Danny isn't a gold digger," Peter said.

"How would you know? He has you wrapped around his little finger pretty damned tight."

This conversation was going off the rails. They needed to reign it in. People in the rest of the office were no doubt overhearing everything Samuel was saying. He wasn't one for volume control. This was supposed to have been a civil opportunity for Samuel to gain some acceptance.

That's not the way it had turned out.

Peter took a seat behind his desk. Perhaps, if they took a seat and relaxed, Samuel would calm down. "I'm moving in with him tomorrow whether you like it or not."

"Like my opinion counts anyway."

"Of course, it does. I want your opinion. You ask hard questions. I like that. You make me think. But at the end of the day, I'm going to make my own decisions."

"Maybe you've got dementia." Samuel slumped into the chair across the desk from Peter.

"You don't believe that."

Samuel shook his head. "No, I don't." He leaned on the desk. "But I honestly don't get it. What you see in each other.

And why you would hook up with one of my friends in the first place. Surely, that crossed your mind. That what you were doing was wrong."

"I didn't kiss him until after we'd been talking for hours."

Samuel's brow furrowed. "You kissed him first?"

"I thought we had made a connection."

"And he jumped at it."

"No." Peter shook his head. "He pushed me away, rejected me, and then we talked until the early morning hours."

"Then he jumped you."

Peter laughed. "No. We parted ways firmly in the friend zone."

"So … how?"

"We were sitting together about to watch a speaker when we decided we didn't want to be there anymore. We wanted to be somewhere else entirely … with each other."

Samuel clapped his hand on his forehead. "Jeezus, Dad. And you just went with him? Back to his room. Just like that … to have sex."

"He was amazing. Caring—gentle. Everything you'd want in a lover."

Samuel's hand slid to cover his mouth. "I don't want to hear about it."

Peter remembered the sadness that had consumed him in that shower after their first time together. "We decided we couldn't see each other again after that."

"Then how did you get from there to here?"

"We couldn't stay away from each other. He showed up at my door saying he couldn't breathe and just needed one more night with me. I felt the same way." Peter folded his hands on his desk and looked down at them. "That was the night he told me he loved me."

"And you believed him?"

Peter looked up at Samuel. "At first, I wasn't sure. But after spending the entire night with him … I knew. I knew he was telling the truth."

"Then *you* fell in love with *him*."

"I was in love with him before he said it to me."

"What? When?"

"Looking back? From the moment I first kissed him in his doorway."

Samuel sighed. "I still don't get it … I don't. And I won't be forgiving Danny any time soon for bedding my dad." He leaned back in his chair. "But with reservation, I'm glad you're happy."

"That's all I needed to hear. I know it's fast. And believe me, I know it's scary. But I trust him. I trust Danny with my life. He's not trying to take advantage of me."

"I'll kill him if I find out he is."

Peter laughed. "Wouldn't expect anything less." It sounded like a conclusion. He breathed out a long sigh as Samuel rose to his feet. He had his son back. He'd lost him for almost a month but now he had him back. His son was happy that his dad was in love.

"I expect to be invited over for dinner once you settle in," Samuel said as he opened the door. "I'll do my best to be nice to Danny. I promise."

Those few words lit up Peter's heart. Samuel was not only accepting his life—he wanted back into it. Samuel was willing to share him with Danny.

Tomorrow couldn't come soon enough.

He wanted to start his life with Danny.

The next day was a bit hectic. The moving truck had been late, and they'd taken a ridiculous amount of time loading up the few belongings Peter was initially bringing with him. It was almost 2 in the afternoon when Peter walked through the front door of what was now *their* home.

Loud voices coming from the kitchen greeted him.

It was a full-on argument between two men. Something about the denying of love.

Peter walked into the kitchen. A beautiful, exotic young man was squared off across the island counter from Danny. He looked familiar.

"You can't deny it … you still love me, Danny."

"You're insane."

The beautiful man rushed at Danny, grabbed his face, and kissed him. Danny was slow to pull away and push the man back across the room.

"Dammit, Dominique," Danny said. "Why now?"

He hadn't heard Peter come into the house. Peter stood quietly in the doorway of the kitchen. Danny didn't sound like he wanted Dominque gone. His heart thudded as he watched Danny walk closer to Dominique. There was a submission in his body language.

Dominique caught sight of Peter. "Who's this?"

Danny turned. A deer in headlights expression on his face. Peter had walked in on something. Something that could scatter their intention to move forward together.

"If you had let me finish," Danny said as he rushed to Peter's side. He grabbed Peter's hand. "I'm with someone." That, at least, was encouraging.

But it felt forced.

Dominque coughed out a laugh. "You've got to be kidding me. Since when do you go trolling for tricks at old folks' homes."

"Peter is not a trick. He's my partner. He's moving in today."

"What … is he some kind of Daddy?"

"Not at all. You know I'm not into that."

"That's true." Dominique winked at Danny. "I remember everything you are into … in detail." He pursed his lips. "Have you shown him your special toy box yet?"

Special toy box?

They'd only had one evening together that strayed away from somewhat spicy vanilla. He was moving in today. He should know what he was walking into.

"We're going to buy a house together," Danny said. He squeezed Peter's hand.

"That's not what I asked … but whatever. I think I have my answer." And then Dominique laughed. A low, sultry laugh. It sent shivers up Peter's spine.

"You need to leave," Danny said.

Dominque pulled out a stool and scooted onto the seat. "I'm not leaving until you kiss me again and tell me you feel nothing."

"You already kissed me."

"And you lingered."

"I did not." Danny looked at Peter and shook his head. "I didn't."

Danny had … he'd hesitated before he pushed Dominique away. A lump rose in Peter's throat. If he hadn't walked in, what would have happened in that kitchen?

He checked himself.

He trusted Danny.

"He caught me by surprise," Danny said. "It took my brain a split second to catch up. I have no interest in him. I don't love him anymore … if I ever did."

That was good enough for Peter.

For now.

"You need to leave our home." Peter slipped from Danny's grasp and headed for Dominque. "You're not welcome here. You heard Danny. He doesn't love you." He gripped Dominque's shoulder. The guy could easily take him. It wouldn't surprise him if Danny told him Dominique was a football player. "I'm asking nicely … leave."

"And what are you going to do, old man? Throw me out?"

"No, but I'm sure the police would."

This caused Dominique to sneer. "I've got enough trouble with them." He knocked into Danny on his way past him. "Think it over. The offer still stands."

Danny rolled his eyes.

It made Peter smile. Whatever Dominique's offer was, Danny was having no part in it. He wandered back through the kitchen and collected Danny in his arms.

He kissed Danny's cheek.

"What the hell was that about?" Peter asked.

Danny sighed. "He wants me back. Offered me a lot of nifty promises."

"Like what?"

"Partial monogamy."

"Partial?"

"A polyamorous relationship with a *super hot guy*." Danny threw a couple of air quotes into the air. "Like that would make a difference somehow."

"Why is that a *nifty promise*?"

"It's something we talked about once."

Peter hugged Danny tighter. "Is that something you're into? Polyamory?"

Danny stepped back to look at Peter. "Not with you. You're

everything I need."

That made Peter's heart soar that he was everything Danny needed. He wanted to be Danny's everything. They were taking a huge risk. They both had to be all in.

"Are you sure?" Peter asked. "It looked like you were headed back toward him."

"Dominique has a way of messing with my head." Danny walked back into Peter's arms. "Honest truth. I have no love for him, but my body still craves him."

Peter frowned. That was quite an admission. The fact Danny trusted him with it lightened his response. His heart was still intact. His love overflowing.

"Where do I know him from?"

"He's a commercial real estate agent."

"Is he going to keep at you?"

Danny sighed. "Probably. Maybe once we buy our own house, he'll realize how serious we are, and he'll back off." He tucked in against Peter's neck. "You're my forever."

In the past couple of days, Peter had deliberately let it slip to other agents that he was moving in with Danny and that was why he had put his house up for sale. There was no going back now.

There were a few long pauses on the phone. A couple of questions. Simple stuff. How long had it been going on? Was this a permanent arrangement? So far, no judgment.

His circle of friends with whom he had once been close were next.

"I listed my house today," Peter said.

Danny smiled. "I found a few properties we might be interested in. The mortgage might be hefty, but I think we can handle it."

Peter grinned. "Right now, there's only one thing I want to

handle."

"If I'm not mistaken, we have movers outside waiting for instruction."

Peter heaved out a long sigh. "You're no fun."

"Oh, but I am. Wait until you see the *special toy box*."

Peter's heart skipped a beat. Since their night of submission, Danny had given him some idea of what he was into kink-wise. It was nothing extreme.

He was excited to see the special toy box.

"As soon as the movers leave?" he asked.

"You'll be getting an education."

"I'll be an eager student."

"Just do what I tell you to, and you'll have that eagerness rewarded."

Peter groaned and tugged Danny into his arms. The kiss Danny landed on him nearly took him out at the knees. It was like a bottomless well of desire.

Desire and profound love.

Chapter Twelve | Epilogue

The living room draperies were flung open to let the light in. It washed the hardwood floors in a warm, golden hue. Peter stood behind Danny; his arms wrapped around Danny's waist. Danny clung to Peter's arms. He leaned back against Peter's shoulder as they both stared out the window. It overlooked a small, manicured yard with two immense arbutus trees.

"Not an ocean view, but this scenery is stunning," Danny said.

Danny had tracked down a Tudor-style home that had rooms with old-world charm complimented with modern features. It was the perfect blend. The house hadn't been for sale, but Danny had convinced the elderly couple who owned it to let it go for something more manageable.

He'd found them an elegant townhome with a strata that took care of everything.

They'd been thrilled to free up some money to travel.

Danny turned and hugged Peter. The house had five bedrooms with ensuites, a powder room, a den, an office, a cozy living room, and a massive modern kitchen with all the eating room they needed. As expected, the mortgage was hefty, but it was everything Danny had ever wanted.

And he got to share it with Peter.

Life couldn't get any better.

Peter pulled away and took a step back—and sank onto one knee.

Danny's heart tripped through a frantic, erratic wave of

beats.

Maybe life *could* get better.

Peter fished a small box out of his pants, opened it, and held it up. A silver band with one small diamond flashed in the light.

"Danny, you have completed me in ways I never thought imaginable. I can't fathom a world in which you don't exist. You are my everything. I want to make that forever."

Tears streaked down Danny's cheeks. He knew how Peter felt about marriage. It was not something Peter would ever enter into lightly. This man loved him—deeply.

Danny moved forward and cupped Peter's outstretched hands in his own. Peter rose to his feet and Danny held out his left hand, fingers extended. "Yes. A gazillion times, yes."

Peter slipped the ring on Danny's finger. "Forever."

"Forever."

Dear Reader

I hope you enjoyed reading *Pacific Pursuit*.

Please take a moment to review this book on the website of the store where you purchased your copy of *Pacific Pursuit.*

If you would like to touch base and say hello to the author, you can email them at: leigh@leighjarrett.com

About the Author

Leigh Jarrett (she/he) is an unabashedly queer, quirky, and passionate author of Contemporary MM+ Romantic Fiction. Their published contemporary works include warm and always sexy HEA romances as well as dark romances filled with grit, trauma, and angst.

In their hometown of Victoria, BC, Canada, Leigh can be found nestled up with their fabulously supportive wife and trusty laptop or enjoying the wondrous Vancouver Island outdoors.

Please consider subscribing to Leigh's newsletter to stay up to date with their new releases and promos. If you're interested in MM+ Fantasy and Paranormal Romance, check out one of Leigh's other pen names, JT Fader, on their JT Fader Fantasticals website and newsletter jtfader.com.

To connect with Leigh Jarrett:

Email: leigh@leighjarrett.com

Website and newsletter: leighjarrett.com

You can also find Leigh on Bluesky

Other Books by Leigh Jarrett

"It all came down to a matter of trust."
A Friends to Lovers M/M Gay Romance
Snowblind

"Find love in the least expected place."
An Enemies to Lovers M/M Gay Romance

Merlot Rebellion

"Risking it all to follow your heart."
A Found Family M/M Bisexual Romance

Capital Adoration

"Learning a new path to love."
A Roommates to Lovers Bisexual Awakening M/M Romance

Academic Adoration

"Recovering true love."
A Second Chance Hurt/Comfort M/M Romance

Drag Undivided

"Strumming your way to love."
A Grumpy/Sunshine Gay Awakening M/M Romance

Rhythmic Bliss